The Red Lily Saga

Volume 1

RIVER SHAYNE

ISBN-13: 978-1-945038-39-6

CONTENTS

WE BLEED

The Red Lily
Part I

CHAPTER 1

LEUKA FALKENER

I never flinched. I didn't even blink as I watched the carnage below. The windows were a nice touch, massive and angled for a perfect downward view of the battlefield. I was right to insist on flying in the older model.

All the commanders in my graduating class were clamoring for the Model Ten. The Phoenix, they called it. My Model Eight had the same multi-angled video monitors as the newer ships, but it also had windows. I didn't want to command an army from behind a video monitor; it felt too distant. Direct line of sight to the battlefield made every decision feel real and immediate and important.

The Model Eight had a nickname, too. The Wraith. Way more intimidating than a damn phoenix.

The dark horde swarmed over the industrialized valley below, like insects over the decomposing carcass of some poor forgotten creature. Smoke billowed up from the burning factories.

"Many will die," I said, half to the pilot and half to myself.

"Not just die. Suffer. The Shadowmen are famously brutal," he replied.

The blood rushed from my already pale face. My muscles pulsed with the desire to act. To inflict violence on something.

Calm. Controlled. Logical, I told myself.

I turned to face the pilot.

"Brutal, are they? And you feel the need to explain this *to me?*"

He shook his head back and forth so fast his white hair whipped across his face.

"I'm sorry, Commander. I'd forgotten."

"You'd forgotten? Funny, I never will." I turned away, my attention back on the broad, angled windows. "Take it in lower. Toward that hill," I ordered him. He shook his head back and forth, his pale face expressionless.

"What hill? We're in the middle of the valley. There's no hill," he said, his eyes darting around the 3D topographical display in front of him.

"I'm looking right at it."

He sighed. The ship did not change course.

"For God's sake, take your eyes off the screen for a second and look out the damn window."

Finally, we began to descend. As we grew nearer, the hill moved, restlessly changing shape. Bits of it dropped off and then reformed. It spun and writhed like a living thing. And it was living. A pile of bodies. The simple Hathor people, wriggling like a pile of earthworms. The dark ones were tossing more bodies on the pile. They pulled men from the building. These weren't soldiers, just laborers in the factories my people had built on this planet.

I spun around to face the video monitors, sliding my fingers from the center of the screen toward the corners to zoom in. Boys, mostly, and very young. Dirty. Bleeding. I saw a man below motion toward the dark army with his hand, and suddenly the pile was ablaze—a wriggling, fiery mass of living flame. Living for the moment, but not for long.

I cringed. I had seen this before, as a child. The Shadowmen had invaded the peaceful desert planet of Rhand, where my father was stationed with the Ministry Army. I could still see the Rhandish peasants lying in bloody piles in the sand. I closed my eyes, but the sounds haunted my memory—the slashing of flesh with dull metal blades, the cries, the bones snapping beneath rocks, clubs, bare hands. I tried not to picture his face caked in wet, burgundy sand. His eyes were as round and green as mine as they fell closed that day. I'd stared at them for hours from my hiding place in the wreckage, just waiting for them to open back up. But they never did.

"Leuka, are you all right?" The pilot looked at me, his face stern and more accusatory than concerned. "If this hits too close to home, given your past, you should step down… for the good of the mission."

I stepped closer to him and stared hard and unblinking into his face. I severed the memory from my mind like a gangrenous limb.

"You will address me as Commander Falkener, sir. It is Fehr blood that runs in my veins. *Emotions* do not inform the actions of a Ministry Commander. Logic, reason, and the greater good. These are the only factors that influence my command. Do you question me?"

"No, Commander. I only meant, you looked… troubled." He took a step backward and lowered his eyes from my stare.

"Troubled?" I stepped forward again and stared at his forehead until he was forced by his own discomfort to lift his head and meet my gaze. "These factories feed and clothe the people of our planet. The Hathor natives supply us with a built-in labor force and the goods they supply are essential for our survival and way of life back home on Fehr. They do things we cannot without the risk of polluting and destroying our planet. Do you wish Fehr to suffer the same fate as Earth? A lifeless, petrified relic?"

I paused. I was about to get too heated, betray emotion that would appear unseemly in a Ministry Commander. I slowly lifted my dainty tin cup to my lips and sipped the lukewarm tea inside.

"These factories are in ruin," I continued. I tried to keep my voice low, my tone and volume even. "Even if rebuilt, who would work in them? The laborers lie dead in burning piles across this valley. And the dark army is inching closer to the satellites that, if destroyed, will lead to our certain defeat in the war for this planet. Are you not *troubled*?"

He didn't respond, just kept staring at me, his face blank. I think he knew better than to look away again. I wouldn't have it.

"I have an army to command. Your job is to steer the ship where I tell you, Pilot," I sneered. "This ship isn't even armed. You're the Ministry's version of a taxi driver. Now take me in closer to the generals."

I turned around without giving him a chance to

respond and took my seat in front of the viewing windows. Another sip of tea and we were moving closer to where our greatest weapon waited, in front of the communication base, prepared to defend our satellites.

The telekinetic generals were Fehr soldiers who had trained their telekinesis to its highest potential for combat. Their skills were incredible, but as we approached I could see their formation was all wrong. I began keying in commands to them through the ship's computer.

"General Hague, triangle formation and I want you at the apex. If they get by you, I want two more waiting behind you, if they get past those, they'll face four behind them—get the idea?"

Hague was the best telekinetic warrior I had ever seen, but clearly not a strategist. He followed orders well, though, and his skill was unmatched. In command school, I saw a vid of him tipping an entire building into the boiling sea on the planet Fierno—a planet so hot it might as well have been on the surface of the sun.

I watched the swarm approaching. They outnumbered my men. Painted in blood and ashes, they looked like an army of the dead, risen to bleed the living dry and collect their souls. Their leader ran along in the middle of the men, not leading or following like most would. It was clear he was in control, though. He was lean and wiry compared to the others. His every step conveyed pride. More than pride. Maybe arrogance. He was a savage among savages, putting on a show of his brutality like he had something to prove. I watched him stomping over the ribs and skulls of the young laborers of Hathor. He led this massacre impatiently. But he commanded with a cunning that extended beyond the unrefined tactics I usually saw in the dark armies.

They were inside a kilometer now. It was time.

"This is it! Attack swiftly and in unison. Keep your distance and don't give up the high ground."

CHAPTER 2

RAELON TOREK

I held the little whelp by his neck with one hand, his feet both off the ground, and squeezed until his eyes rolled back. Then I tossed his body into the concrete wall of the factory and did my best to ignore the sickening crunch, like dry twigs snapping underfoot. *Pawns,* I told myself. *Just pawns of the enemy.*

"Leave these." I spit on the burning pile of Hathor laborers and when I spoke, my men stopped in their tracks and looked to me. "Onward. Our enemy awaits."

They weren't easy to command. Especially for me—an outsider, a half-breed. They were mountains, each of them, with the classic, muscular build of the Shadowman warrior that my father shared. But my mother was an outlander peasant from a conquered planet. I was born leaner, taller, faster than the others.

They saw my mixed blood as a weakness. But it never was that. It made me fight twice as hard—I had to be better. Soldiers are trained from early childhood, tested with violence by their own kind. Only the strongest survive to fight the real enemies. For a half-breed like me, it was worse. They came for me in my sleep, as I bathed, when I wandered to the woods to piss. Came for me in number and with weapons. But I had survived, using my differences to beat them. I was smarter. But intellect didn't gain you respect among the Shadowmen. They honored strength above all and held no regard for mercy. I had earned my place with every jaw I broke and every nose I bloodied with bare fists and elbows. Some of them still doubted, but most of them were mine—endlessly loyal and unquestioningly obedient.

"There are still laborers inside. Shadowmen leave no survivors!" It was one of the newer recruits who dared speak against my order. The others looked to me with fear in their eyes for this man, awaiting my reaction in electric silence. I loved seeing that look.

"Open the door," I ordered the young warrior.

He slid the iron bolt out of place and threw open the factory door.

I picked up the fuel oil we had used to burn the bodies soaked the inside walls and floors until the last drops trickled out.

"Bolt it shut."

I heard the iron click back into place as I walked toward the pile of burning bodies. A foot stuck out from the pile, as yet untouched by the flames consuming the rest of the body. This one would do. I moved fast, grabbing it by the ankle joint, spinning and hurling at once. The young soldier ducked, the flaming corpse barely missing him as it flew inches above him and crashed through the first-floor window of the factory. It ignited and in seconds the building was roaring in flames. I smiled.

"Satisfied?"

The young soldier rose from his crouching position and brushed the dirt off his pants.

"You heard him, brothers. Onward," he yelled as he broke into a run toward the enemy generals.

I ran, too, staying in the middle of the group. I liked to stand with my men, not lead them from the front or trail behind for my own safety, like so many warriors. I needed them to think of me as one of them.

"Stay close, tight formation."

The men fell in closer as we ran, our footsteps pounding a rhythmic beat against the valley floor. A chorus of screams emerged from the factory as the fire engulfed the higher stories and fell against our backs as we ran.

Ignore the sounds, I told myself. But they would stay with me always. The screams I had collected, the blood and tears, they were mine for this lifetime and those that lay beyond.

"Our enemy would put you down without touching you! Will you let them?"

"No!" the men howled in unison.

"They mean to slaughter us with weapons fashioned from the bones of our own people! Will you let them?"

"No!" they called again.

"We may share ancestors in the ancient men of Earth, but the pale ones are not our brothers! They carve knives from our bones because theirs are weak and frail."

The men grunted and cheered their agreement.

"Crush them!"

The first attack was imminent. I could see the generals. Damn, the enemy was already in formation. We faced down a triangle of telekinetic warriors, the strongest, no doubt, at their apex. Some commander must have recognized the idiocy of their earlier row arrangement. They would have been far easier to defeat that way. But it didn't matter. We just had to get within arm's length. The Fehr were weak. Hand-to-hand, we could defeat them outnumbered ten to one. Telekinesis and intellect made them dangerous.

The first general raised his arms and, with them, dozens of knives floated in the air. The other generals imitated his movement and in seconds, we were running full speed toward hundreds of flying blades. About half my men went down in that first wave.

The generals lifted their arms again and, with a sickening sound, the blades tore out of their victims' flesh and flew backward in the air, poised for a second attack.

I reached down and pulled two struggling warriors to their feet; Tor, one of the few Shadowomen warriors in the horde, and Rhef, a gentle giant of a man, brave, simple, and loyal to a fault. They were bleeding, but would fight on, I knew. They were the best of my warriors and had been by my side since I first took command four years ago. I would drag them on until the bitter end, and they would fight until the enemy was no more than dust and ash.

"Use the dead to shield yourselves!"

I hauled a fallen comrade up from the dirt and held him in front of my torso by the waist of his pants and the neck of his shirt. It was the young soldier who had questioned me earlier. Good. One less to doubt.

Tor heaved a body up off the ground, grunting. Sweat ran down her face, leaving rolling trails down the blood and ash that colored her brown skin. Her matted masses of dreadlocked hair were gathered on the unshaved side of her head and bounced with every heavy step she took.

The others followed my lead as well, but many of them weren't as fast or coordinated. They couldn't move well with a corpse shield—it was cumbersome and awkward. Shadowmen weren't known for their grace. Rhef struggled, lumbering forward with a body held against his chest in a bear hug. He fell a few paces behind before groaning loud and throwing the body aside in frustration.

The once-white knives were smeared in deep red as they flew again. This wave was devastating. Warriors dropped all around me, the ground shaking with the impact of these falling titans. They cut our diminishing numbers in half once more. I pushed on, glad Tor and Rhef were still by my side.

As the bone knives tore out of the fallen, a mist of blood showered over us and our tan skin was painted a rusty red-brown.

"Wear the blood of your brothers as war paint! Fight with their vengeance in your heart!"

Two blades caught me in the next wave. One just below my collarbone and another stuck between two of my ribs. My comrades paused when I fell. There was less than a dozen left.

"Push on," I growled from the dirt. I flung the dead body off me, hard and far. I had to show them I was still strong. I took one of the bone knives in each hand and ripped them out of my muscle and flesh. The pain coursed through every fiber of my body. It hurt in my teeth, but I grinned like a madman at the soldiers I had left.

It was over as soon as we reached them. They didn't panic. That could be said for them. They held to formation and kept pushing with the attacks, but at this range they couldn't get a single knife in the air before we were upon them. They panicked, attempting to push us back with their telekinesis, but lacked the skill. It was one thing to move a small inanimate object, but another thing entirely to push an army of moving beings as they fight your will with their own. Only the general in front of the formations had the strength to succeed in this and he couldn't take us all.

I could feel his intent like a living being, pushing us, pushing me. But I would not be moved. Two of my soldiers flew over my head, writhing in the air. Their grunting screams faded as I charged forward. Their wills were weak.

I lifted the first general I saw off the ground by his head, my thumbs finding grips in his eye sockets. I used his body as a club and smashed the two behind him. Their bones crumbled like porcelain. It was too easy. I left the rest to my men and ran ahead. The satellite was what mattered. And that could not be left to just any Shadowman brute to handle. I would take this myself.

I climbed the surrounding wall with ease. The bulkier warriors wouldn't have the agility for this anyway. I could see the satellite about a kilometer away, in the center of this walled military compound. I turned to look back at my soldiers from the top of the wall. Tor, Rhef, and a handful of others were laying waste to the pale generals, tearing fists full of their white hair out, scalp and all. Limbs snapped, eyes gouged, all brutally audible with the cracking, popping, splashing. It was a deadly orchestra. I could have leapt over the wall, but then I saw it.

First a Ministry spacecraft spun out of control, passing just feet above my head. I dropped to my belly, barely retaining my balance on the narrow wall top. It crashed in the distance, somewhere. I looked up to see where it had come from.

"Shit."

A tidal wave of flame was hurtling toward us from the hills above. Seconds. There were only seconds. I might be safe on the other side of the wall and I could still complete the mission. I looked back and saw Tor and Rhef staring wide-eyed at the wall of flame.

"Go," they screamed at me. "Finish it!"

CHAPTER 3

LEUKA FALKENER

"They're through," I said. "Their leader is at the wall. Where are the reinforcements?"

I looked to the pilot, who had been mumbling softly into his headset.

"We have ten more generals leading small battalions at the other side of the valley. They're eight minutes out."

"We don't have eight minutes."

I watched their leader, his wiry, blood-soaked body climbing the outer wall protecting the com sat. His hair was dark and long, matted to his forehead with blood. I had to get him off that wall. He wouldn't be stopped otherwise. I had watched this beast pull two knives out of his chest with a smile on his face, and continue fighting.

"Tell them to take down the dam. It will flood the valley. It's our only shot at stopping them."

The entire crew stared at me, unmoving. Not one of

them spoke in answer.

"What are you waiting for? Tell them!"

"Commander, if they take down the dam, they and all the rest of our troops in the valley, and any surviving civilians will be killed. It will wipe out every military unit down there. Only those beyond the wall will survive," the pilot said.

"There are thousands beyond the wall. It's in the words of the Ministry. *For the good of the many.* We vowed this when we signed up. This is what it takes—give the order."

He shook his head, staring down at the valley, his wide eyes on the viewing monitor.

"I won't do it. I won't order them to kill themselves. Not to save the damn natives."

I yanked his headset from his head.

"I'll do it myself."

I threw the headset on. It hung lopsided and was too big, but I didn't care.

"Blow the dam! Do you copy, they're breaching the wall. Blow the dam, it's the only way!"

Silence for a moment. Nervous, static, silence.

"Are you mad? We'll all be killed!"

"The whole planet will go down if you don't. Just take down the dam."

I watched on the video monitor as my generals each removed their earpieces and tossed them to the ground in defiance of my order. Weak, frightened, children.

"Fine—I'll do it myself. Take us in closer to the dam," I ordered the pilot.

"This ship isn't armed. You can't shoot it down. "

He floated us in closer, just above the dam. The dark leader had reached the top of the wall.

"Left—over the factory to the left of the dam. Good."

I sprinted to the emergency controls. First, I pulled the lever to eject our fuel supply. This was a built-in safety feature to use in case the ship caught fire. It helped avoid a big explosion if you could land quickly—not a good idea if you had any distance to travel though. The fuel rained down over the factory and dam below us. I could see it, glistening and iridescent on the surface of the water.

"Take it lower. Hover just above the furnace room."

This ship was equipped with back-up engines. If an engine blew, the back-up would take over and the pilot could eject the failed engine to decrease the overall weight of the craft, increasing speed and power. Our engine was still running, but if the goal was to cause a massive explosion, it would do quite nicely.

I hit the engine eject button and it was almost instant. The heat hit us like we were inside an erupting volcano. Every metal surface inside the ship was burning hot. The ship rocked to the side, picking up speed fast. The pale faces of my crew were lit with the orange glow as their eyes and mouths widened in terror. For the briefest of seconds, we were all in the air, the ship spinning around us as we hung in some strange trick of gravity between the walls and floor. The ship lunged downward and I crashed into the ceiling. I looked to the others, but I seemed to be the last one conscious. The ship flipped once more and my body slammed flat against the glass windows of the viewing deck. I saw the spider web cracks creeping across the window, slow and quiet. Then all was black.

CHAPTER 4

RAELON TOREK

I felt the wave of heat nearly push me over before I saw it coming. I had never seen anything like it. A tidal wave engulfed in flame. Hell was racing toward me, ready to swallow this valley and everyone in it. My training told me to complete the mission. Take down the satellite. I would be the lone survivor, battle scarred but honored and victorious among the warriors of my world. If Tor or Rhef had been on this wall instead of me, I had no doubt that they would carry on and complete the mission, gain the glory and win the day for our people.

But they weren't on the wall. They were below me in the valley, about to be drowned in a burning sea. I jumped back down from the wall and grabbed each of them by whatever I could catch in my haste—Rhef by his shirtsleeve, Tor by a handful of her dark, dreadlocked hair.

"What have you done?" Rhef shouted. "You've lost the whole planet!"

"To save both your lives," I spat, dragging them behind me as I ran.

"It will cost you your own. Fool," Tor said. Her words were harsh but her voice was a groaning whisper.

I shut it out and kept running. My mind was busy calculating how to get us out of this damn valley before it became a lake of fire. Dragging the two of them was like pulling two fully grown bulls by their nostrils. They couldn't keep up, couldn't push their thick muscles and heavy bones any faster. So I pulled. With everything in me, I pulled.

The river was the only way. If we could reach it, we might be able to get downstream to safety before the fire took us. I pulled harder. Some of Tor's dreadlocked hair was ripping from her scalp in my hand. No time to be gentle. I grabbed a bigger handful and kept going.

My knife wounds were pouring blood. I felt the sticky wetness dripping down my torso, my shirt sticking to my chest and stomach. The heat licked at my back like a cat's rough tongue as the fire raced nearer. I didn't look over my shoulder. That would do no good. We would make it or we wouldn't. The river was close now. I stumbled on the boggy ground, but I was close enough. I threw Rhef and Tor so hard a shockwave of pain coursed like lightning through my arms and chest.

It was then that I looked back. The fire was almost upon me. It was a thing of unnatural beauty, so captivating that I almost let it drown me in its impossible fiery depths. Opposing forces. They should cancel each other out. But here they were, entwined in some deadly embrace so fearsome and powerful it seemed it could swallow me whole.

I stumbled forward, flopping down over the bank into the river. The cold soothed my wounds and I let myself float downstream in the rapid current. I closed my eyes for a second, but I fought the exhaustion, blinking until they stayed open. I latched onto a fallen tree, black and charred from the explosion, as it drifted downstream.

"Tor," I called. "Rhef!" They were nowhere in sight.

I lowered my head. Had I killed them? Had they drowned when I threw them in the river? Shadowmen weren't strong swimmers. They were often too dense to float.

I gasped when Rhef popped out of the rushing water, reaching up with one arm to grab hold of the log. He grunted loud and heaved Tor out with his other arm, pulling her to the log as well. I smiled.

"Hang on, Boss," Rhef whispered.

I felt big hands pull me up higher on the log as my grip began to falter. I felt my eyelids drooping, and there was only cold, wet, and pain.

CHAPTER 5

LEUKA FALKENER

I opened my eyes and saw the muddy ground floating below me, as if I were levitating where I lay, held up by a spider web. It wasn't until I opened my mouth and metallic tasting water rushed in to fill it that I realized I was under water. The spider web beneath me wasn't a real spider web at all, but a cracked pane of glass. Blood spiraled around me like ribbons, dancing through the water as it diluted, becoming paler and paler pink. The blood of my crew.

I held my breath. The bodies appeared serene, drifting about the flooded ship's cabin. They floated above me like phantoms. Eerily calm, my dancing dead. And they were mine—after all, I had killed them. All of them. I owned this destruction.

The cracks on the window crept outward, ever more links in the great web. My telekinesis was never as good as that of the combat generals, but I focused hard until the cracked window burst outward in a sparkling explosion of glass shards. I swam out from beneath the ship with my eyes open, though the dirty water stung. My body ached from the crash, but I had survived. That was more than I could say for the rest.

My chest burned as I struggled for the surface. Above me I could see patches of glowing orange. The fuel, the explosion. The surface of the water was still ablaze in places. I searched for a safe spot to emerge, aiming for darkness among the glow and hoping for the best.

When my head broke the surface, the air was foul, laced with the smell of chemical accelerants, smoke and death. The sun was setting, adding to the eerie orange glow of the sporadic fires on the surface of this newborn lake. I had avoided emerging in flames, but instead found myself surrounded by cold, white, floating bodies. Fehr generals. My generals. I had condemned them to this fate.

Swimming was near impossible, the spaces between the dead too small to fit through without touching them. Shaking, despite the fire-warmed water, I pushed the bodies aside and dragged myself through. I kept my eyes down, afraid to look at their faces, their blank, staring eyes.

"Stop it," I snapped at myself, my voice shrill and unnatural to my own ears. I glanced around, my self-conscious mind awaiting a reprimand for my emotional outburst, but of course none came. The valley was silent except for my own voice and the crackling of dying flames. This is just what they would expect from me—weakness, tears, whimpering and shaking. I pictured my mother's face, cold and stony as they lowered my father's body into the ground. It was a great honor, she had told me, to be buried in the Capitol of the empire, the city of Dega. The highest ranking military officials were present as well as several Ministry Councilmen and women. A great honor, indeed.

I had screamed then, hot tears pouring unashamed. A child, I kicked and punched, my tantrum known to any within shouting distance and I didn't care. The tall trees shading the cemetery had bowed to my rage, bending under the force of my telekinetic fury until their tallest limbs kissed the soil.

I hated my mother for her shame over my outburst and for her coldness. Didn't she care that he was gone? Didn't she feel that the world had ended that day? I hated her more for letting them claim his body for the military, like he belonged to them more than us. Now he would be worlds away from our home on the planet Fehr, just another stone in another row identical to all the rest.

But I wasn't a child anymore. I understood now the way of our world. Emotion is weakness. Don't let it color your mind. It will pervert your logic and make you hasty and stupid and careless. I closed my eyes for a moment and breathed the harsh dead air. Then I pulled the two bodies in front of me close together—latching their stiff arms around each other to keep them close.

I had some difficulty with them—stiff as they were. A snap or two, something dislocating inside, and then they were hitched. I crawled onto their backs and rode my dead soldiers to the place where the lake was spilling blood and flame and countless corpses into the wide mouth of the river.

The water was colder as I floated on downstream. The sky was growing darker. Stars peeked out of that clear cold sky and I noticed they were the same pale yellow-white as the hair on my corpses, spreading gently across the surface of the water and rippling in its bubbly waves.

I froze when I heard deep voices. Male—not Fehr males though—they were too low and sinister. Shadowmen. They must be survivors. I slunk down into the water with one arm and one leg hooked around my companions, hoping that I looked as dead as I felt.

"The satellite?"

"It's out of reach now. There are three of us, and we're injured. They'll have reinforcements by now. We regroup with the others and I will face my failure."

"You'll lose your command for this, if not your life. You should have let us die. Most would have."

Not all men. This one sounded female, though her voice was deep and ragged.

"I acted on instinct."

His voice was barely a whisper. But so cold and stern it felt as if the water dropped ten degrees as soon as it met my ears. I heard a noise and opened my eyes to see a hulk of a man and a woman who would have easily made two of me. They were hunched over, their four arms wrapped tight around a third, smaller man. I had never seen people embrace like this. I shivered in the arms of my dead companions, realizing this was the closest I had ever been to a Fehr man. Even my father had held me only once that I could remember, as he lay dying in the sand. Fehr men did not express this kind of physical affection, even to their wives and family. Shadowmen were the last beings I ever expected to see showing gratitude or loyalty.

"What was that?"

I shut my eyes tight and slumped back into the water. It wasn't fast enough. They were approaching the riverbank as my companions and I drifted nearer. My kneecaps dragged against the muddy riverbed as the water became more shallow. We slowed to a crawl.

"Bodies. Pales."

Pales. That's what they called us. We were much fairer of skin and hair than the Shadowmen. Most Fehr were blond with pale colored eyes and the whitest of skin. I was a rarity with my strawberry tinted hair, though it was still quite light. There were others like me, but we were the minority. And fewer still with green eyes like mine—I inherited them from my father. Our eyes were identical oddities among our people, dark and green and bright.

"Make sure they're dead."

I could hear the squishing of mud and grass beneath heavy footfalls. They were almost on top of us, but I kept my eyes closed and didn't move. I felt a jostle as someone kicked one of my companions. An audible crack sounded when one of them kicked me hard in my side. I didn't move. I felt the urge to gasp for breath as the pain raced down my nerve endings. But I didn't make a sound.

"Dead. Looks like two generals and a little girl," one of the gruff voices said.

Little girl? I was a goddamn *commander* with twenty-six years since my birth. But for whatever reason, people always believed me to be a teenager. My features were soft, not sharp and narrow like most Fehr women. I had more curve to my body and fuller eyes and lips. And I was short. But I didn't care. I was stronger than them, too, in any way that counted.

"Dead for sure?"

"For sure. Let's get back to camp."

CHAPTER 6

LEUKA FALKENER

I awoke in a white room. White women in white clothes surrounded me like the angels in stories from the old world. But angels they were not.

The ceilings were high and ornate, with little swirling patterns repeating over and over. I'd never been in such a place. All stone and columns and bright white light, sharp and artificial. It made the pale skin of the women attending me glow with a sallow tint.

I sat up in the narrow bed, wincing at the pain that shot through my ribs.

"No, lady. Rest. You'll need your strength. You go before the council soon."

"Where am I? What planet is this?"

"Tokino, my lady. You are in the city of Dega at the headquarters of the Ministry."

The other nurses came nearer, one on either side of

my bed. They each took one of my arms and sat me up straighter. I complied, though it was painful. For some foolish reason, I wanted to smash their heads together. Illogical. They were no threat to me and we shared no conflict. My pain was causing an emotional response. Anger. I pushed it down into my swirling gut and sat still, dead-eyed and passionless. The ideal Fehr citizen.

The nurse who had spoken bound my waist with white bandages tighter than the corset my mother had tried to make me wear to the military gala when I was fifteen. That horrid silver corset. It had cut into my skin, squeezed so tight I could barely speak above a whisper. And for what? To flatten down my breasts and hide the curve of my waist? To make me look like the other Fehr girls, all gaunt and willowy. I had cut it off with Father's filet knife and thrown it into the fire. But that was another time, when I had been another girl entirely.

The room had no door, just a curtain beside my cot… for modesty, I supposed. Footsteps approached, soft at first but growing louder. The curtain began to shift. I looked down at my bare arms and crossed them over my chest.

"Where are my clothes?"

"They were destroyed," a white-haired woman answered as she entered from beyond the curtain. "But the council has provided this for you. A garment suitable for a Fehr lady."

She held a white gown, beautifully draped, backless and asymmetrical. It was lovely.

"I am not a lady. I am a commander in the Ministry Armed Forces."

"And I am a councilwoman, activist, and advocate of the people. A woman can be more than one thing."

The corners of her mouth turned up as she spoke, bringing out the wrinkles on her worn skin.

I bowed my head to her, ashamed.

"Councilwoman, forgive my rude words. I didn't know."

"Your words were true to you. Do not edit them because I sit in a larger chair than you." She turned to the nurses. "Leave us."

They scurried out of the room with their eyes down. I was impressed by the authority this old woman wielded.

"Dress, child. Dress and listen. I won't let you go into the pit of vipers unprepared."

"Pit of vipers?" I pulled back my covers and stood up. My head began to spin. I focused hard. Do not falter, do not tremble. Stable. Strong. I stepped into the dress and pulled it up around me, slow and deliberate.

"The Ministry Council. Snakes, the lot of them. They'll underestimate you, child, and you'd do well to let them."

"I will take whatever punishment I have earned for my actions, and take it with honor as it is bestowed upon me by the Ministry Council. The Ministry works for the greater good of all planets and beings. And if I'm not mistaken, you are one of those *snakes*, as you call them."

She smiled. "I'm called Avia. I'm a councilwoman in name only. The true power lies in the hands of a few. I have as much say in policy as your handmaiden."

I hooked the silver clasp on the back of the dress.

"I don't have a handmaiden."

"Oh. You will before the day is through."

"Are there handmaidens in the prison colonies?"

She laughed, loud and abrupt, then snorted softly. "You're not going to prison. They don't want to punish you. They plan to reward you, or at least make it look like they did. Your legend has already spread over all three systems. The Triad will not miss an opportunity to use this to their advantage."

I bowed my head. "I will serve the Ministry in any way they request. I trust in their wisdom."

She shook her head. "Yes, I expect you do. You may come to me at any time. I am not like them. Keep your eyes open, my dear. Things are not always as they seem."

She turned to leave, but stopped at the edge of the curtain and spoke with her back to me.

"If your faith in this 'greater good' begins to falter, do not let on. Bad things happen to those who speak against the Ministry."

Her whispers echoed in my head as I walked down the long, narrow corridor to the council chamber. It was more like a theater, the seats rising high above my head and filled with hundreds of councilmen and women. A pit of vipers?

I caught myself listening for the hiss, the slither, the rustling of dry scaly skin being shed and left behind. But my own footsteps were the only audible sound, echoing to the far corners of the great room, announcing my entrance. I looked down. A thousand pairs of eyes were trained on me. Were they glaring? Blaming me for all those lost lives? They should be.

My mouth fell open stupidly when I saw the digital images floating across the walls. Me. Countless images. Training at command school, leading in battle, even one of me floating among the bodies from my disastrous victory at Hathor. My skin began to crawl and I felt the eyes on me, heavier now. But they weren't just in this room. The Ministry had eyes everywhere. I realized at that moment that I hadn't been alone for even a moment since I'd joined this army.

The crowd was a sea of white. I couldn't make out individual faces, so I let them melt into a blur at my periphery. The sea rose as Minister Chrogus entered, surrounded by his three closest advisors—the Triad, they were called. Together, they were the four most powerful people in the universe. And I was about to stand before them to explain why I had let three thousand soldiers die.

The Minister sat front and center. The Triad moved as a unit, careful not to sit until just after the Minister. They were all dressed in gray, except a young woman I'd never seen before. She wore black, making the shock of her pale skin and hair stand out that much more. But who was she?

Reasor Harris sat directly to the right of the Minister. He was familiar and strange to me all at once. A legend, known less by his given name than the nickname he'd earned through years of combat. Stone Fist, they called him. He'd been a member of the Triad for longer than I'd been alive. I'd studied him. A brilliant military strategist and one of the only Fehr in history to have beaten a Shadowman warrior in hand-to-hand combat. His face was as hard and cracked as the stone desert on Hathor. As if my thoughts were audible, he raised his head and looked down at me, eyes cold and gray and ancient. I lowered my head, a chill sweeping through me.

I stood awkwardly in front of the Minister and the Triad, my back to the crowd of councilmen. I was the only one standing. There was no chair. Should I sit on the floor? Or kneel? Maybe I should bow? I had never stood before the Ministry Council. Someone should have given me etiquette lessons. I could feel the heat rising in my face, probably coloring my cheeks.

Then the Minister beckoned me forward with a soft snap of his wrist and a smile that, coupled with his white hair and receding hairline, made him look like a kindly grandfather. I tried to walk with confidence, like the woman in those pictures floating around the walls. The man to the Minister's left was smiling as well. His name was Benedict Vaughn, but in my head I just called him "Teeth." He hadn't stopped smiling since I first saw his face. It made me uneasy, feeling that bright smile beaming down on me like a spotlight. I had never seen a picture of Benedict Vaughn in which he wasn't smiling that shark-toothed grin. I guess people found it charming. They spoke of him often. Women called him handsome. I found it reminiscent of the fluorescent lighting in a dentist's waiting room. I knelt before them on one knee, lowering my head toward my thigh.

"Rise," the Minister commanded.

I stood.

"We have all heard of your heroic victory over the dark armies at Hathor. I have convened the Ministry Council here today to honor your bravery and commend you on the sacrifice you made for the greater good."

He nodded to the strange young woman who stood behind Stone Fist, her hair shimmering an iridescent reflection of the artificial lights overhead. She was pretty, in a way. Like a sickly baby bird. She held in her hands a wooden box. I recognized it. My father had one just like it, except it had been dust coated and resting up high, on a shelf that I was too little to reach.

"To do you this honor, I present the newest member of the council, and my most recent appointee to the Triad, Miss Reed Silvernail." There was a quiet muttering in the crowd as the Minister's words echoed. Stone Fist stood, and as his eyes fell on the crowd, the whispers died.

"Miss Silvernail, you honor your father's memory by serving in his place," he said. He took her hand as she stood, eyeing the crowd again as she passed him.

She stood before me, presenting the box and lifting its hinged lid. The medal inside gleamed a brassy-gold, the image of a red flower on its face.

"The red lily is the rarest flower known, growing only on the north hillside of the distant rocky-rim planet, the Gol. It symbolizes uncommon bravery and self-sacrifice. The Ministry Council presents you with this medal—created uniquely for you. It is one of a kind."

When she finished speaking, Reed pinned the medal on the left side of my dress, just above my heart. It was beautiful and heavy. I didn't look at it; I wanted to put it back in the box and hide it away.

I raised my head to thank them, but all four were staring above me. I turned. High in the middle of the crowd, one tiny councilwoman stood from her seat. She seemed to be in her late thirties, but may have been much younger. Her face was aged by dark puffy circles around her bloodshot eyes. I'd never seen her before, but she looked like she would have a kind face if she stopped glaring. She didn't stop. She kept her narrow, red-rimmed eyes pinned on my own. I thought she might be crying, but she was too far away to see for sure.

"Be seated, Councilwoman Breach," Stone Fist called out. "You are interrupting our proceedings."

"I will not," she called.

"Councilwoman," Benedict addressed her warmly. "You've been through much this week. Perhaps you should recuse yourself from Council. Your head is clouded, dear. You're not thinking logically."

"You will not silence me with your false concern, you grasping little sycophant. I will have my say."

Benedict smiled and looked over his shoulder at Stone Fist. Fist nodded.

"Guards, have her removed," Benedict said, the smile still on his face like it was carved there with a hammer and chisel.

The guards filed in from their stations at the entrances of the chamber. They weren't Fehr—there were not enough Fehr warriors to go around, so the Ministry trained natives of occupied planets for local armies and personal bodyguards. It was a prestigious position for the natives, to be a part of the Ministry Guard.

"You honor her for murdering our soldiers. My husband. My son. You took them!" She was shouting at me now. Pointing a long, shaky finger. "If you are so brave and honorable—why are you alive while the men you commanded are all dead? You should be executed, not honored!"

Stone Fist stood from his seat, his eyes fixed on the woman. She froze for a brief second and then collapsed, her bony figure slumping to the floor.

I forgot myself for a moment—where I was, to whom I was speaking. I looked at him and shouted, "What did you do to her?"

The tiniest glimmer of a smile shone on his lips before he responded.

"Do? She's simply fainted, overcome by her illogical emotions and probably suffering the soul sickness. Fear not. They're removing her now, you see?"

One of the Ministry Guards tossed her over his

shoulder like a bag of flour and filed out of the chamber with the rest. Business as usual.

"What will happen to her?" I asked.

"You are speaking out of turn, young one," Stone Fist said. "Do you question the actions of the Ministry?"

My eyes widened. I couldn't speak. I heard Avia's words in my head. *Vipers.*

Benedict's voice broke the silence. "Our young hero is new to council proceedings. She is just concerned for that poor foolish woman. I assure you, Commander, Councilwoman Breach will be taken care of. Now let's get back to business, shall we?"

He looked around, smiling warmly at his companions. The calm was eerie. Everyone was still. Utter silence. The disturbance had never happened. The councilwoman had not existed.

Minister Chrogus stood. He looked over the audience. Nothing about his face looked kind or grandfatherly now. He looked at them like a watch dog, surveying his territory and ready to rip out the throat of any creature that dared move in his terrain. Then he faced me again and as he spoke, his face reverted to its previous form, round and rosy cheeked and smiling once again.

"As reward for your brave actions, you are being appointed to the post of military strategy consultant. You will work directly alongside the council and the Minister's Triad on a number of special assignments." The four of them began to applaud and the other councilmen and women immediately joined in.

When the noise died down, Chrogus continued, his voice cheerful. "An estate has been set up for you here on Tokino—fully staffed, of course. Reasor has personally selected men from the Ministry Guard to protect you from sunrise to sunrise. Unless there is any other business, I will adjourn this convening and allow your guard to escort you to your new home. It's outside the city in Desert Edge."

I started to open my mouth, to protest. I was no bureaucrat; I was a commander. But out of the corner of my eye, I saw Avia perched in a high seat in the crowd. Her lips squeezed in a thin line. Her face was flat and devoid of expression. But in her eyes burned something that was dying to get out. She moved her head from side to side, so slowly it was barely perceptible. I bit my tongue hard and allowed my new personal guards to whisk me out of the chamber and into the narrow corridor.

They marched so fast I struggled to keep up. I tried to stop once but they pushed and pulled me along, surrounding me on all sides, manipulating my movement like a potter with soft clay. Finally, I threw out both my arms, striking the two on either side of me in the chest.

"Stop!" I shouted.

They all stared at me. Dammit, I needed to control my emotions—they were too dangerous. Especially here.

"I need to use the restroom before we continue."

They nodded at me. Creepy. How they moved in unison. Pulling me along to the bathroom door, they were so close to me that if I stuck my tongue out I would taste the salt of their skin. They stood so near the door that it hit their captain firmly in his thigh as I swung it open. *Should've swung harder*, I thought.

I watched the door close behind me before crossing the room and standing at one of the porcelain sinks. I turned the gleaming silver handle as far as it would go and watched the sink bowl fill with clear, cold water. I wanted to scream. To curse and thrash my limbs and break every object within my reach. I wanted to punch the mirror until my knuckles bled, the way I had when I was a foolish teenage girl and my father had died. Instead I stuck my face in the ice-cold water with my eyes wide open and held my breath until my chest burned.

Then the door swung open, its hinges singing out their warning. I whipped my head backward, splashing the wall behind me with the cast-off from my soaking wet hair.

"You look ridiculous. Here. Dry off."

I blinked the water from my eyes and saw Reed Silvernail standing before me, a towel extended in her bony white hand. I hardly believed it was her. I'd seen her face years before in the news posts back on Fehr. The Silvernails were one of the wealthiest and most influential families on the planet, and as such were frequently featured in various forms of media. But Reed, the youngest Silvernail child, had all but disappeared from the news posts for the past six years. Rumors circulated that her family had disowned her and she'd run away to the outlying planets. My mother always said gossip was undignified. She used to read every scandal rag she could get her hands on with desperate, hungry eyes before feeding it through the shredder and labeling it as "indecent."

"Thank you," I finally answered after seconds of awkward silence. "I was just…feeling a bit overheated."

I took the towel and patted my face dry, glad for the excuse not to meet her pale gray eyes. But when I looked, her eyes were still pressed upon me like a cold steel blade.

"Congratulations again," she said. "Your father was also given a medal for his service, was he not?"

"He was."

And for the first time, I was glad he was no more than bones buried in a pretty box. Glad he couldn't see what I had done.

"You honor his memory," she said.

I wanted to ask her about Councilwoman Breach. That poor woman had stared at me like I was something from her nightmares. And I was. I was a ghost. I'd died for the mission. I'd made the sacrifice play, the act of valor, or whatever you wanted to call it. I wasn't supposed to live. I was never supposed to live with what I'd done.

"Are you all right? You look ill."

"Fine, Miss Silvernail. I was sorry to hear about your father. My condolences."

Her head cocked to one side, eyes big and blank and gray, like a psychotic baby doll.

"He was alive. And now he isn't. What's there to be sorry about?"

Her arm twitched as she fiddled with something deep within her pocket.

I wondered, for a moment, if she had a soul.

"I mean…he *was* your father," I said.

"And?" she said.

She patted my shoulder once, her arm stiff, like she didn't quite know how to perform such a gesture. Then she strode out of the room without using the toilet or even one of the sinks.

I looked up at my dripping face and hair in the little round mirror. This was reality—the sunken eyes, red rimmed and circled in dark blue-gray. Weak. Wounded. Afraid. Not the crisp black and white images the Ministry had projected, floating billboard sized around the walls. That woman looked cold and sharp, sure of herself and her duty and her place. I wasn't sure I would ever feel like that again.

The medal hung heavy on my chest and pulled my sweaty clothes away from my skin. I yanked it off, tearing the front of my formal white dress, and slammed it on the porcelain sink so hard I could feel the bruise forming on my palm. Fool. *Control yourself*, I thought. We bruised easy, my kind. I was lucky I hadn't broken a bone.

They couldn't fool me with their praise. They wanted a poster girl. Word had spread fast and anything to increase the popularity of the Ministry would be used. I would be used. The new face of the Ministry. I didn't want anything to do with it. I cursed under my breath and bit my lip.

The door swung open a crack and the captain of my guard poked his head through. "Everything okay in here, Commander? I heard something."

He eyed the tear in my dress and his hand floated just above the long handled sword at his side.

"Are you from a planet where privacy in the bathroom is not a reasonable expectation?"

"I'm from this planet, Red Lily."

"Don't call me that." I failed at maintaining a civil tone of voice.

"But that is your designation."

I didn't turn to face him, but kept my eyes on him in the mirror. "What are you called?"

"Captain Soldes, my Lily."

"Who trained you, Soldes?"

"The Stone Fist."

"And did he teach you to follow orders?" I rested my palms on either side of the sink, leaning my body weight against it.

"Yes. He taught us to follow orders above all else."

I turned to face him now.

"Then what is wrong with you?"

He stared at me in silence.

"I order you to answer me. What is wrong with you?"

His mouth opened and shut silently, eyes darting around the room.

"Are you broken? Answer me, soldier. What is wrong with you? Because you haven't followed a single damn order since you walked in here."

He opened his mouth again but nothing came out.

"You and your men are dismissed, Captain. I don't need babysitters."

His eyes snapped up and he became suddenly stern.

"Apologies, my Lily, but that's not how it works. You have been appointed to work for the Ministry. As Ministry Guard, we were assigned by the Stone Fist and the Minister himself to watch you at all times. They are the only ones who can order us to abandon our post."

"Are they the only ones who can order you to get the hell out of the women's bathroom?" He did not respond, just turned and let the door swing shut behind him.

CHAPTER 7

RAELON TOREK

We walked north, until Hathor's rocky forested foothills gave way to the barren Stone Planes of the north. Bone dry and cold, the gray rock floor of this place was solid and void of life. No soil, no plants, just unyielding dust-colored rock. I ignored the pulsating agony from my mud-crusted stab wounds. I was not forcing myself on with willpower alone. It was almost the opposite of that. Some things you cannot fight. I hurt. But that is the nature of pain. Pain hurts. My legs carried me on through the sand, step after step just by muscle memory. Pain hurts. Legs walk. Heart beats. Until it doesn't—and at that point, I won't be worried about it anymore.

Tor and Rhef were on either side of me, their arms just inches from mine. I walked in silence, breathing in the chill, unencumbered wind and cursing each time it bit at my clammy flesh.

The rock mesa shot out of the flat stone floor, high above our heads in the distance. We were close. My footsteps were smaller with every step, closer to the ground, shorter. My body was tired, but I walked on just the same.

The spiral of wood smoke circled overhead like so many vultures. The drums were already sounding in the distance. The Alpha had heard of my failure. There would be no explanations, no argument. It would be the blood ring.

I approached in silence. They were gathered in a circle already, waiting eagerly for the entertainment to come. Moses sat above the others, the jutting angular rock beneath him echoing the harshness of his squared jawline and prominent brow bones. The others surrounded him, staring. Their eyes were wide with fear, or maybe excitement. But the Alpha's eyes were on me. His most skilled warrior. His greatest threat. Shadowmen are governed by strength, not position. If one were to step up and defeat him in combat this very evening, he would command the same respect and fear that Moses now held. It had been years since anyone had dared challenge him.

He stood as I approached, his bronze body solid and angular as the rocky mesa beyond him. He towered over the rest, one of the few Shadowmen as tall as me, though the rest of his body was bound in thick muscle, bulging from beneath his tan skin.

I held his gaze. My companions quickened their pace as we grew nearer. The circle parted for us and we moved into the center. Tor stepped ahead of me, forcing her body between me and the Alpha. The little hairs stood up on the shaved half of her head and neck, like a territorial canine. She spoke fast and unbidden.

"The Blood Ring? He saved our lives and you'll see him slaughtered for sport?"

"He betrayed our cause with his actions. And must prove that he deserves to keep his life. Unless you choose to fight in his place, girl? I'm sure there are plenty of warriors who'd love to get their hands on you."

She stepped forward.

"You're damn right I will," she shouted.

I pulled her back toward me and took her place in front of the Alpha.

Rhef stepped up now, his arm falling across my chest as if to hold me back. "He is injured from battle. Half drowned and exhausted. At least let him rest."

I silenced him with a look and stepped past him.

"I require no rest. Who will it be?"

I walked around the inside of the circle of warriors, sidestepping so I could face them toe to toe. Brawny monsters, most of them, and hungry for the blood sport. They craved the excitement of the competition, but I doubted any of them wanted to take me on—even injured as I was.

"Choose who you will, Moses. Or fight me yourself." I addressed the Alpha informally, and made sure the others heard me.

The crowd buzzed.

"Do you dare challenge me for the spear, half-shadow?"

I let the electric silence stretch on. I wanted them to think about it, to see the fear in his eyes when he considered the possibility of me challenging him for the right to rule.

"No. Just inviting you to challenge me. If you think you're up for it."

My mouth curled up at the corners in a grim smirk. I wasn't pleased to have to kill another man, but I would not be beaten. The fight was already beginning, between my mind and theirs. Knowing this was my advantage.

I pulled off my blood and dirt-crusted shirt and tossed it in the fire roaring at the Alpha's feet, exposing my back to the firelight. A reminder. Their eyes were quick to find the scars that rested across my back from shoulder to shoulder. Five symbols, branded into my flesh. Five times I had walked into the Blood Ring with another warrior. And five times I had walked out alone.

I felt him before I saw him, like a swirling nausea in the pit of my gut. Bishop. Once a warrior like myself, he now preferred killing without all the trouble of a fair fight. Moses's personal assassin, enforcer, errand boy— he was pathetic, cowering close to power. He glared at me from where he stood, close at the Alpha's right side and half bathed in his shadow. I sneered at him with no attempt to hide my disgust.

I leaned in close as I approached him, so our foreheads were inches apart. "Bishop, I pray the Alpha gives me the pleasure of your company in the ring."

"One day he will, that's a promise. But on that day, you'll never see me coming," he whispered.

"That's right. I'd forgotten, you prefer to fight from the shadows these days. Tell me, when's the last time you hit a man who could hit you back?"

I jumped back when I felt sharp little legs scurrying over my arms and chest. I flung them off with the back of my hand. The scorpions fell at Bishop's feet and, one by one, began to melt back into his body as if they had never existed. He laughed.

"Always in the company of vermin. Don't you have any human friends?"

His eyes flashed wide for a moment, then I felt another of his creatures crawling over my neck. I snatched it off without looking and tossed it into my mouth as if it were a bite-sized morsel of rare meat, crunching it down with my teeth until I could taste its venom spilling onto my tongue. Just when it began to sting, I spit it into his face.

He wiped at his eyes and face, but a streak of angry red appeared from his left eye across his temple and into his hair line. He took a forceful step forward and reached toward me.

"Enough!"

Bishop snapped to attention at the Alpha's growl. My heart was pounding so hard I could feel it in my ears. Good. Adrenaline. Blood flowing hard and fast. I was ready.

"Gage. You will face Raelon in the Blood Ring."

Gage stepped forward from Moses's left and turned to face him. We knelt, side by side at the Alpha's feet, and the ritual began. The drums grew louder, pounding in time with my pulse. We kept our heads down as the circle was prepared—this was customary. The other warriors walked the perimeter of the ring three times. At the completion of each lap they sliced their right palms with a blade, spilling blood along the boundary of the circle.

The drums stopped.

"Rise."

As we stood, the Alpha reached forward with both hands and snatched the gleaming metal symbols that hung at each of our waists. The spirit sign. The symbol of honor given to each warrior who has earned the right to lead in battle. Each one of a kind.

Moses pinned our signs on his shoulders and pushed us into the ring. I walked in step with Gage. Focus. Clarity. There is no opponent, I told myself. I am my opponent.

We hooked elbows and bowed in the center of the ring.

"Begin."

Gage bounced around, moving his massive frame back and forth as if to create the illusion of agility. Wrong. He should be conserving his energy. I tried not to betray my awareness with a smile.

I circled him slowly, moving only in reaction to his movements. It was a waiting game at this point. I moved, light and slow on the balls of my feet. Like a coiled snake, lying in wait.

He swung. Hard, but slow. I swatted his hand out of the way. A mosquito.

He threw again. Too high. I ducked beneath it.

He kept swinging. I reacted without thought, blocking each strike as it came. The nighttime desert air brushed my cheek, cool and pleasant, as I bent my head from side to side, dodging, weaving. A moving meditation. I had no plan in my head of when to defend or attack or where to place my feet or what stance to use. I just moved, limbs loose, feet agile, never crossing.

My awareness was supernatural. I heard his heartbeat quicken and his breathing become shallow. Rapid. I watched his cheeks turn pink in frustration.

He punched low. I blocked hard. Downward. Climbing his body with forearm blocks until his arms were pinned down. Fist struck, his chin snapping back.

Face red now. Nostrils flaring, the metal ring he wore between them vibrated with the movement. I could see his breath. It moistened the night air as he pushed it forcefully from his mouth.

He struck again, fast and wild. Jab. Jab. Cross. Block. Block. Duck. Too hard on the cross. He was off balance. Counter. My body reacted before my mind was even aware. Hard kick to the knee. Another to the hip bone. Paralyzing shot. His body stiffened for a second. Long enough. Execute. I threw my hips into the hook kick, my body snapping like a whip. My foot met the side of his head and the sound was sick. Crunching, snapping. His face mangled and broken, he fell to the ground. His neck was twisted unnaturally to the side.

The onlookers cheered for blood. I was ashamed of the pride I felt as his contorted body twitched in the sand. My body shook. I stood, arms out, playing the crowd. They couldn't see me shiver. I wouldn't survive that. So they never would.

"Finish it! Finish it!" they cried out, thirsty for the death blow.

I circled the broken body. Blood was already seeping from his ears, the corners of his mouth. I pulled him to his knees and took each side of his head in my hands. With one swift jerk, I snapped his neck. His body fell back against me. I wanted to cradle him in my arms, wash his blood away with my tears. Instead I dropped him to the ground where he could be still.

My hands were painted in his blood. Shadowman blood. The blood I shared. It sickened me, the blood. But I could never let them see that. I pressed my dripping hand across my face, leaving a bloody handprint.

The crowd roared. Ashamed of myself, I fed on their energy. I jumped to my feet, pounding my chest and roaring out loud.

Moses stood from his throne of rock and all fell silent. "Kneel."

I knelt with my back to the Alpha and my head down.

I could hear the metal shaft snapping into place as he fit it onto the back of Gage's spirit sign. I kept my eyes closed. He would be heating it in the fire now. I'd seen it before. Watching only made it worse. The anticipation of the pain to come. The metal glowing brighter and brighter, like a dying star at the center of some galaxy. *Be still*, I told myself. *Be silent.*

I couldn't help but open my eyes, just once. The metal sign was glowing red-orange in the flames. I squeezed them shut again.

Pain. Searing hot, scalding pain. It began at my back, just below my neck and a little off-center. Then it spread through my nerves and I couldn't tell where it hurt. It just hurt. I kept my jaw clamped shut and held my body still. Don't shake, don't fall. I had seen men faint from the branding before. I would not be one of them.

He pulled the metal from my back and the cheers sounded again. The cold water poured over me, a shock to my scalded flesh. I stood, spun around slowly, showing the mark to the crowd. Now an even six brands decorated my back from shoulder to shoulder. I liked the brands, though the pain was immense. They intimidated people. A status symbol, earned by survival.

I knelt before Moses again, a custom I hated. As far as I was concerned I had no superiors and was superior to no one.

"Alpha, I have proven myself in the Blood Ring. May I have the honor of resuming my command and leading my brothers in the next battle?"

He smiled.

"No."

I stood. I could feel the blood rush into my face. The silence was heavy.

"Haven't I proven myself?"

"You have earned your life. But your failure cost us dearly in the war we wage. You must redeem yourself for this error."

"How?"

"The Fehr Commander who beat you. Bring me her head. Until then, you have no home among us."

I shook my head. "She's no threat to us. The battle is over."

"They're all a threat to us! Every last goddamn pale is a threat to us. Their empire is expanding daily. Do you recall that we weren't always a nomadic people? That we once had a planet? A homeland? Until the Ministry was formed. Until they came to show us simple folk the ways of advancement. And polluted and destroyed the place we called home."

"Shadowrock was dead before anyone here was ever born," I said. I was out of breath and cold, though sweat dripped from my forehead and rolled down my face and chest.

"You pledged your breath to me, boy, the day you earned that spirit sign. The girl's head. Or exile. You may choose," Moses said with finality.

I nodded solemnly.

"As you command."

CHAPTER 8

LEUKA FALKENER

I wanted to walk down a corridor and hear only my own footsteps. I wanted to eat a meal alone instead of under the constant watch of a dozen armed guards. Everywhere I went, they followed. From the moment I woke up at dawn and began my physical training, their eyes were on me. I began to wonder if they were there for my protection or to keep me prisoner.

The glass-paned door creaked as I eased it open and felt the low morning sun on my face. My handmaiden sat up from where she was lying on my sofa, sleep in her eyes and a soft smile on her face.

"Awake already, my Lily?"

I grated my teeth at the title, but let it go. Cece had been kind to me since I'd arrived at the Capitol and I would not alienate her. Instead I forced a smile, which felt strange and foreign on my lips. But somehow nice.

This simple exchange of emotions.

"Shall I start your breakfast, my Lily?"

"I'll train first. And I've told you before, I can cook my own meals. I've no need or desire to be waited upon."

Her smile spread over her tan face to form little wrinkles around her deep brown eyes.

"Yes, and that's what makes you so fun to serve. Go on and roll your eyes, but it's true," she said. I hadn't realized it, but I *was* rolling my eyes as she spoke. My back had been facing her, but she could still tell.

"What did you do before the Ministry came here? Were you a handmaiden to someone here?" I asked.

She laughed, shaking her head. "I was a pilot."

My mouth fell open and I stared at her stupidly, unable to respond.

"Just a local post. Mail deliveries. Farm supplies to the desert and such."

"And why aren't you a pilot anymore?"

She looked at me, shrugging, as if I should already know the answer.

"All the locally owned planes and crafts were destroyed when the Ministry arrived." She poured fresh orange juice into a glass and placed it in front of me. "You must at least drink before you train," she said.

"Why don't you join me this morning? I could use a good sparring partner."

"Me, my Lily? Not one of the guards?"

"You. If you're not afraid?"

She smiled, the light twinkling in her eyes, and pushed past me out the door. I jogged out behind her.

My feet dug into the soft, warm sand at the edge of the reservoir. Desert Edge was beautiful. The mirrored surface of the reservoir stretched out for miles, reflecting the pale blue-gray of the sky overhead. In the opposite direction, the desert seemed endless and eternal. Just sand and rocks. Here and there a cactus rose through the sand, maybe a twisted leafless tree. They fascinated me, the plants that grew out there. It was so barren, so void of anything that nurtured life. And still they grew.

Cece often painted the horizon with homemade oil paints on slabs of stone while I trained at sunrise. Reds and blues she ground herself from berries, flowers, even insects. As beautiful as her paintings were, nothing could capture the stark and solemn beauty of this place. Perhaps I was being ungrateful. The Ministry had granted me this promotion, placed me in this beautiful estate bordering one of the rare bodies of water on the planet. This reservoir housed the water supply for the entire city of Dega. The house was beautiful, too. Open, spacious. It had everything a soldier could possibly need to train for combat—both telekinetic and hand-to-hand.

I still preferred to train outside, when I could. The gear was nice; the facilities were perfect. But my body was the only tool I really needed. I had always trained this way, and it had kept me alive this long.

"Form. Execution. Repetition," I said. "These are the principles of my training."

Cece nodded, following my body with her eyes. My every motion was fluid, blending with the next like a dance. The techniques taught in the military were fierce. Deadly if done right. But I had always found them beautiful. My fists flew with deceptive speed. I kicked hard and accurate, stretching my reach to capacity, making use of every inch of my limbs.

Cece stood behind me and mimicked my movements clumsily. She giggled with every error she made and eventually flopped down on the sand in defeat.

"You are very good, my Lily. Most Fehr don't fight so well with hands. They fight only with their magic."

I collapsed down beside her. It was rare that I took a break during my training, but today I just wanted to feel the cool sand against my back.

"It's telekinesis. Not magic. And no, the Fehr are not known for hand-to-hand combat skills. But my father always taught me to train my weaknesses the hardest. It's a good way to stay alive."

She wrapped her thumb and forefinger around my wrist, holding it up above her head weakly.

"But you're so breakable. Isn't that true? The Fehr, not just you?" She released my wrist and I let it fall to just above my face, twirling my hand back and forth, examining for weaknesses.

"It is true. Our bones are naturally brittle. Weight-bearing exercise can strengthen them to some extent. And building muscle around them can help to protect them. Still…we all break at one time or another."

I slid my palm down over my still-healing ribcage.

"But broken or no, you still train, still work. Still go on," she said.

I nodded.

"I know something about that," she said.

I hopped back to my feet and extended a hand to help her rise.

"Ready?" I asked. She shrugged, then nodded. "Attack me."

Cece ran forward, swinging her arms wildly. I gave her pointers on technique, blocking her punches gently but never striking back.

"You fight much kinder than the guard."

I stopped mid-counter and let her palm strike me in the cheek.

"Oh, my Lily, I'm sorry." She dropped to her knees.

"No, Cece, I'm fine. When have you ever had occasion to fight the Ministry Guard?"

She looked over her shoulder, where my dozen body guards stood at attention ten yards away.

"It's okay to tell me."

Her face hardened.

"You are kind, my Lily. But you are still one of them."

Sweat had soaked through my cream bandeau top and the moist fabric sent a chill over my hot skin. Hours had passed and the red-gold sun was rising above the water, coloring the morning with a warm glow. I wiped the beads of sweat from my forehead and began to stretch. But I wasn't done with this discussion.

"Cece, I'm not done talking about this."

She looked up at me, then back toward the guards and to me again. Her lip was trembling.

"How can someone like you serve them? The things they've done to us."

Behind us a door swung closed. Before the sound of it died I had spun to face it, arms raised, a dozen freshly sharpened bone daggers hung motionless in the air awaiting my command. Cece covered her mouth with both hands.

"Excellent reflexes, my lady. Your telekinesis is growing quite advanced." The blinding white smile beamed like a fluorescent bulb, clashing with the soft morning glow. Benedict Vaughn, member of the Minister's Triad, but I just referred to him as "Teeth." Not out loud, of course.

I lowered my hands and the daggers floated to the ground, like they were part of me.

"I owe it to the army to get better. The most talented telekinetic warrior to ever fight for the Ministry Force was General Hague. And I killed him."

The Teeth looked around, as if taking in the scenery.

"Lovely place, though sparse on decorations. I imagine you're still unpacking. Are you enjoying it, so far?"

I glanced at the door behind him, focused hard and flung it open from twenty feet away. He jumped.

"I've unpacked. Travel light. What is it you wanted? Or are you truly here to discuss my home decor?"

I walked past him, through the open double doors and into the huge common room, Cece beside me, walking in step. The guards were instantly at our heels and stood in front of us like eager puppies as we sat on the edge of the hard sofa.

Teeth came in behind them, and sat on a tall metal stool by the countertop. He gestured at a file folder that lay on the counter.

"Handmaiden, you're dismissed. We have Ministry business to discuss," he said.

Cece's face hardened. "You do not dismiss me, Sir. I work for the Lily, not you," she snapped.

He turned to face me, plastic smile intact.

"It's okay, Cece. Would you mind preparing some tea?"

She nodded at me, but paused for a long moment, staring at Benedict with narrowed eyes. She didn't trust him. Neither did I. But he was no danger to me; he was simply a sycophant, clinging close to the powerful. She stood and scurried out of the room, light on her feet and graceful.

"From the Minister. There is discontent among some of the Tokino natives. The laborers are becoming restless in the factories of Dega South. And the peasants and farmers in the rural areas are blaming us for the failure of their crops. As if it's our fault they are trying to farm a desert."

"I don't understand. We are taught on Fehr that natives rejoice when the Ministry arrives to their planets."

He stood, pacing back and forth in front of me. "The Minister is concerned that there may be an uprising. As you have gained quite a lot of popularity across the Empire with your heroism. He thinks they may respond to you as a voice of reason."

I could feel the crease between my brows deepen as I narrowed my eyes. "What will he have me do? I suppose I could tour the factories and take inventory of conditions and labor practices. I could address the workers' complaints, and make changes if any of them are founded."

His smile faltered briefly, then softly reappeared. He placed a hand on my shoulder.

"I think it is best that you leave the factories to myself and Reed Silvernail. The Minister wants you to be more diplomatic. Use your image, you know, mingle with the common folk and gain favor. And as you do, try to gain information. Are they organizing? Are they skilled in any sort of combat and do they have an arsenal of any kind?"

I shook my head and cast my eyes away from that glaring fluorescent smile towards the polished cement floor, cold and hard beneath my bare feet.

"They will be more receptive if I am actually addressing their complaints. I can't address them if I don't know what they are. I'd like to see the factories."

"The factories are not your concern. You have your assignment. The Minister will send me back for a full report, so I suggest you begin immediately."

His sudden sharp tone caught me off guard. But in a flash, that smile was back on his face and he was shaking my hand.

"We are truly blessed to have you among us on the Ministry Council. Good luck and, please, if you require any assistance, don't hesitate to contact me or the other members of the Triad."

I pulled my hand from his grip.

"We're not done here," I said.

He stood still as a wax figure, the smile on his face not touching his hard eyes.

"What about Hathor? The Shadowmen have abandoned the planet in defeat. We must begin the effort to rebuild."

He shook his head.

"There will be no reconstruction on Hathor. The Minister has determined that the cost would be too great. Good day, Lily."

He started to turn for the door but I grabbed him by the shoulder and forced his body back around to face me.

"So it was for nothing? All those people. For nothing?"

He sighed. "A significant percentage of the planet's resources have been utilized. And the labor force was cut by thirty percent from native casualties. The dam powered everything. When you blew it up, you effectively cut the legs off our industry, agriculture, and military in one fell swoop."

I dropped my head. He said something else but my ears were buzzing, like I'd stuck my head in a hornet's nest. By the time I looked up, he was walking out the door.

I squeezed my eyes shut, trying to keep my composure.

But I could feel the red seeping up into my normally pale cheeks and forehead.

Cece poked her head out from the stairwell.

"It's not true, my Lily. It wasn't for nothing. The Shadowmen would have taken the whole of Hathor. Burned it black just because the Ministry wanted it. You saved a world. Maybe not your own world, but you saved it just the same."

I could hear her, but she sounded far away. When she touched my arm, I flinched. I felt raw, burnt and raw and sensitive to the point that feeling anything at all was intolerable. If only these damn guards would leave me alone for a minute. I wanted to break something. Impossible, being composed all the time. The surge of anger welled up like a rock in my chest. So much pressure I thought my heart would burst. Then it felt like it did. A shockwave of energy pulsing out of me all at once. The giant bay windows in front of me shattered in an explosion of sparkling glass shards. They rained over us. The guards ducked and covered their faces. I was motionless. By the time they stood back up, I was stomping away. I snatched the little file off the counter, marched into my study, and slammed the door.

CHAPTER 9

RAELON TOREK

I flew the whole damn six-hour trip to Tokino crammed in the tiny "stealth model" aircraft, my knees nearly touching my ears. Four hours of sleep. Still aching from the battle. It would have been more comfortable to crash into the sea and swim to shore. And that plan sounded more than reasonable to me, in my current condition, but I had to keep the ship functional in case the need arose to make a hasty departure. Ship—if you could even call it that. I kicked the brown metal interior wall.

I brought her down in a massive expanse of dull gray sand. Nothing around for miles except a few falling-down barns and shanties. Probably abandoned. What was once a self-sufficient, though simple, farming economy had fallen apart when the Ministry colonized. They pulled all the water into the massive reservoir and pumped it into the city they'd built, the factories they ran and profited from.

I climbed down through the little round hatch in the floor; exhaling as I squeezed through it was the only way I fit. I tumbled out gracelessly and somersaulted onto the forgiving sandy floor.

The nearest structure was an abandoned barn just over a mile to my west. For the first time since I had climbed into that ship, I was glad it was so small. I hooked the rusty tow chains to my belt and started off for the barn. Tokino had some nasty sandstorms, especially since the water had been sucked out of the sand to feed the city. I would need cover for the night and a place to hide my ship. The closest barn would do. As long as it didn't collapse on me. With this particular barn, it looked like about a fifty-fifty shot.

The moon was setting. The dark night sky was growing inky black. Tokino's moon disappeared from visibility at about midnight—plunging the world into pitch black until the sun rose hours later. The exact time varied by the phases of the moon, but it ranged anywhere from two to five hours. I pulled a flash orb from my satchel and cracked it on the side of the ship before blindness set in. The neon green glow spread in spider web cracks around the sphere, casting its eerie light over the desert. I oriented it above my head and a few paces ahead of me. I took three steps forward and watched it float, mirroring my movement. I took a few steps back and it followed. Satisfied that it was functioning, I started off again across the lonely desert.

The barn didn't come into view until I was just a few yards away, the weathered wood dim and green under the light of the flash orb. A rolling door stretched across the front wall, sparse chips of paint cracking off in places, though it was impossible to tell what color. I threw it open too hard, surprised by how easily it slid on its tracks. A metallic bang punctuated my overexertion. As old as it looked, it should have been rusted shut. I dragged the ship inside. The cool night air burned as I breathed it in. Fast but not deep. The deeper I inhaled, the more my lungs expanded and stretched the stab wounds on my chest and ribs. I had cleaned them well before leaving, but they still burned with every move.

I unhooked the tow chains and let them fall to the barn floor with a dull clang. The sweat on my torso appeared sticky in the orb light, like bile mixed with tar. Not sweat. Blood. They must have opened back up.

I pulled the door shut again. It was heavier than it should have been. Sweat seeped from my neck and back. Every beat of my heart felt like a bass drum banging inside my ears. I flopped onto my back on a stack of old hay bales. They were itchy against my sticky skin. I closed my eyes. I blinked them back open. The orb. I've gotta put that light out. But my eyelids were heavy. Heavier than the ship I'd dragged across the desert, heavier than the ancient barn door. Too heavy to hold open any longer.

I awoke to the sharp stab of steel pressing firmly against my groin. The blurry outline of a little girl settled into focus, silhouetted in the dim green light. As I began to move she pressed the dagger down harder.

"I'm damn quick with this knife, mister. You can test your luck if you want, but ain't many in this desert that would bet against me."

THE END

WE BOW

The Red Lily
Part II

CHAPTER 1

RAELON TOREK

For a moment I thought I was still unconscious, the images around me little more than a fever dream. The skinny girl in front of me silhouetted against the dim green light of the flash orb was just a bit of a thing, all knees and elbows. A ponytail hung high on the back of her head and bounced every time she spoke.

"Well this is a weird thing to hallucinate," I muttered to myself. Beads of sweat rolled off my top lip to salt my dry tongue the moment I opened my mouth.

"No such luck. I'm the real thing, sunshine."

She leaned forward and I felt the pressure of cold steel push firmly against my groin.

I looked down. Tiny hands glowing in the green light. With tiny fingers. Wrapped around a knife so small it looked like it was made for her.

I exhaled and raised my hands up. She eased back the pressure a bit. Her little hands looked bizarre, gripping that grown-up weapon with white-knuckle force.

"How old are you?" I blurted.

"Old enough to know what men are usually looking for when I find them skulking around here at night. Now why are you in my barn?"

"I'm a merchant. I was heading to Dega on a trade mission, but I crashed in the desert and needed shelter. I'm injured—you see, from the crash."

Her eyes fell to the bloody wounds on my chest and ribs, narrowed, and returned to my own.

Before I could blink she was behind me, the dagger pressed tight against my neck.

"Yeah. You're injured all right. And that might be the only honest word that came out of your mouth. That ship ain't big enough to carry merch for any productive trade mission, buying or selling. And it don't look crashed to me. Piece of shit, but I 'spect it came that way."

She poked me hard in the abdomen and I flinched despite my best efforts. "And these are stab wounds. Been cleaned up, scabbed over and reopened—probably a day old at least. Not from a crash. You're as much a merchant as I'm a damn ballerina."

I stared at the kid. She looked about eleven years old. Kids weren't usually so...

"Mister, you've got one chance to convince me you're not another slaver scum come from the city *recruiting*. Now I killed the last two slavers come 'round here. Stabbed the first through the heart with this very blade." She paused to wiggle the knife she held at my neck, for emphasis. "The second one got the jump on me, but he was stupid. Could'a just dragged me off but he was a man. So he hurt me first. The worst way a man can hurt a girl. Thought I'd just cry in a corner while he pulled his trousers up, tied his boots. Well I picked up a rock no bigger than my fist and I hit him and hit him until the white sand was red and he had a face his mama wouldn't know. Did her a favor, you ask me."

I wouldn't blame her if she killed me right here. If I were her, I already would have. Why was she even giving me a chance to explain? Dumb kid. Her compassion could get her killed.

"Why would I have a ship? If I came from the city to abduct girls and bring them back to the city, why would I need a ship? I promise you, I am not one of the monsters you've described."

She paused. Her face went soft for a just a second, then right back to stone.

"You don't look like a slaver. Don't talk like one either. So then what are you doing in my barn and why shouldn't I slice that pretty fat vein in your neck?"

"Artery."

Her head cocked to one side.

"It's an artery in my neck that your knife is trained on."

"You ain't helping your case."

I shrugged, trying not to smile. She might kill me in the next five minutes, but I couldn't help but like this girl.

"My people are at war with the Ministry. I'm here on a military mission. That's why I'm hiding. If you leave now and keep silent, I will be gone by daylight and no harm will come to you."

She blew out a gust of air through closed lips.

"If I leave now, you won't survive until morning. You're bleeding out as it is. If by some miracle these wounds don't kill you, the Shankers will roast your flesh on a skewer before daylight. They can smell blood kilometers away—like sand hounds. Only, I'd rather face the sand hounds."

"What do you care? You're going to slice my artery anyway, right?"

She pulled the dagger away from my neck and leapt up off the hay bale so fast I fell backwards, my head thudding against the hard straw.

"The Ministry stole my father from us. Worked him to death in one of those factories. My brother is still missing—probably dead, too."

"I'm sorry." And I truly was.

"Shit happens. You can stay out here if you want, keep your ship here. We don't have a lot of food, but I'll share what we do have. And you should let me fix up those wounds. I'm good with a closure gun."

I looked down at the wounds, still oozing blood each time I breathed. I sat up to look her in the eye. "Okay," I said. "But why are you doing this?"

"Lay down, shit-for-brains, you're making it bleed more. If you're after the Ministry, you're welcome to stay. And I can tell you're not lying about that. Don't try that shit, either. I'll know."

I nodded. I wouldn't try to lie to her again. Honesty was the only tactic that had worked in my favor.

"I've got some of Dad's old clothes in the house."

She stood and I started to get up to follow her, but she turned around quick and shoved me back down. It was far too easy for her to push me. The barn's interior rocked back and forth until it was a green blur.

"You can stay in the barn but you will not come to the house. It's my mother and me alone. Trust me when I say that if you put a damn finger on either one of us, I will set you on fire while you sleep, and watch you burn alive.

Now—I'll go get those clothes and my closure gun."

She scampered off into the darkness quick, like a freckled little kitten. I could have run, but the kid was right. I was losing blood, and every move I made seemed to push it out faster. For the moment, she was the best bet I had.

CHAPTER 2

LABORER A-4992

Pink stained fingers. They didn't mean the same thing they used to. Two years ago, pink stained fingers meant berry picking in the wild briar patches. It meant leaving home with a dozen other farm kids like me and returning with buckets full of fresh berries, red and ripe and dripping and sweet. Our legs and arms all covered in scratches from wading waist deep in the thorny berry patch, we still returned smiling, with as much of our bounty in our stomachs as our buckets. What we didn't eat we'd give to the mothers, who'd bake us treats enough to feed an army—the kind that left our little houses smelling warm and delicious for days.

Pink-tinted fingernails, red streaks beneath them. Now it meant blood. And that's all it meant.

The "enforcers." That's what we called them. Their fingers were always stained pink. Shirts too. Splattered in it. Blood. Our blood. On my first day here, I had learned this was a law of nature. The sky was blue. Their fingers were bloody pink. That kind of blood just never washes off.

The boy next to me was nodding off on the work bench. I nudged him with my foot under the table. They'd hurt him if they saw. Especially if he dropped the expensive piece of machinery he was assembling. Then they'd use the rope on him.

He startled awake when my foot struck him in the shin. His big, almond eyes popped open, blinking away the sleep, those impossibly long, dark eyelashes fluttering like the legs of a spider. He was so young. So small.

"Thanks," he said. "They just brought me here from aeronautics assembly. What's your name?"

"No names here. Makes it easier," I said, my voice barely above a whisper. I glanced around as I spoke, keeping an eye out for the enforcers.

"Makes what easier?" the little boy asked.

"When the guy next to you drops dead of dehydration. When the guards come in and take people away. If you don't know their names, it's easier. Easier when they don't come back."

The kid brushed his hand through his dark brown hair, his freckled face wrinkling up as a big yawn stretched his mouth wide open.

"My daddy died in the last factory. I couldn't not know his name though. He's my daddy."

"You can call me A," I whispered.

"Okay," he said, his face softening into an almost smile. "You can call me L."

"Shhhhh," I urged him, letting my head fall forward to stare again at the metal and wires in my hands. But I wasn't fast enough. The enforcer was stomping down our row, his boot-clad feet pounding the filth-stained stone floor between the work benches.

"If you're talking, you're not working," he growled, cocking his fist back over his right shoulder.

I don't know why I did it. I knew better. Knew what would happen. But the boy couldn't have been more than ten. His skinny arms shot up to cover his head as the enforcer wound up to strike. As his fist flew toward the boy, I caught it in one big hand as I stood from my bench. I'd always had big hands, long arms and legs. I was clumsy, growing too fast for my own good, but at fifteen I was already taller than my father had been last time I'd seen him.

The rope hit me from behind. I expected it, though I didn't see it coming. I dropped his fist as I fell forward to my hands and knees on the stone. It was thick. As big around as my balled-up fist and it ripped through the cloth of my shirt as it struck my back again and again. I kept my eyes on the stone floor, looking for patterns in the swirling red-brown stains. It hurt. But it was the same old hurt I'd known almost daily for two years.

When it finally stopped, I brushed my hands off on my dirty jeans and hurried back to my seat at the work bench, my shaky fingers fumbling with the tiny pieces of wire.

The boy looked over at me, his eyes wide. He didn't speak. His hands didn't stop twisting the tiny screws into the metal tube he held, though they trembled just like mine. I looked at him for just a second, nodded once, then returned to my work.

Liberty Rhode

"Don't call me Libby. It's Liberty. Liberty Rhode. Pop's the only one I let get away with that and he's in the ground."

I grunted and kicked hard at his kneecap. He blocked the kick easily and paced a wide circle around me in the sand.

"Suits you. Kick was all wrong. Play to your strengths, not mine," Raelon said.

"That kick was textbook—exactly how you taught me."

"I told you once, kiddo, no whining. I agreed to train you on that one condition, but I'm no babysitter."

"Sorry." I continued circling, then threw a quick three-punch combo followed by a jumping roundhouse. He avoided my strikes with ease.

"Better. But more. What are your strengths?"

I groaned and kicked the sand. "I don't have any! You're stronger, bigger, and you've got a better reach."

"Quit pouting or we're done."

I straightened up, tucked my lip back in and raised my guard.

"Good. You think the slavers that come for you will be smaller than you? Weaker? Use your size. Fight inside and move fast. So fast they can't overpower you. Let them think they've got you pinned—you're weak, remember? They'll use that. You use it, too."

He backed me up until I was against the wall of the barn and swung a hook toward my jaw. I ducked underneath him and threw a hard back kick, striking him in the back of the thigh just above the joint. He dropped to his knees for a second, and then hopped back to his feet with all the agility of a desert panther.

"That was perfect. You're a sneaky little bastard," he said, grinning. "Speaking of which, where have you been sneaking off to at night?"

I twirled my hair, trying to think of an answer. Trying not to look like I'd been caught.

"What are you talking about?" That was the best I could come up with? Weak.

He picked up his sweaty shirt and shook the sand out of it before wiping it across his tan forehead. There were lines on that forehead that shouldn't have been there. People always said I looked young for my age. I was small, lean. Most guessed I was ten or eleven instead of my actual thirteen. But Raelon looked old for his age. Maybe not old, but worn. As if each of his twenty-eight years had been as heavy as two or three. His forehead wrinkled up even more when he looked back down at me.

"No? I've been here a few weeks now."

"Three," I interrupted.

"Three weeks now. And every night since I've been here, you disappear right around the black hours. It's never until after that light goes out inside the house. So wherever it is, I'm thinking you don't want your dear, sickly mother to know about it."

I stared at him hard, tears forming at the corners of my eyes.

"I just gotta get away sometimes. She's so sick. And it's just me now. I can't keep her safe the way my brother used to. She can get a paper cut and bleed out a pint before it stops. Sometimes I just need a break." I sniffled and looked toward my toes in the sand.

He lay his big hand on the middle of my back.

"For a human lie detector, your skill at deception is pretty damn pathetic."

I shook free of his hand.

"What's it to you, anyway?"

"Listen, kid, you can go out stalking slavers all you

like. But the minute you cross that line and gut one with those knives I know you carry, you bring a world of trouble down on both of us."

I spun on him.

"You followed me!"

He shrugged. "Well, yeah."

"You got a problem with my extra-curriculars, go find someone else willing to hide a Shadowman on a Ministry planet. They're as scared'a you as they are of the Shankers."

He was silent.

"I didn't know you knew."

"Well duh. You fight like them. And the scars are a dead giveaway."

He brushed his hand over his upper back, touching the raised scars like a blind man reading braille.

"Doesn't change the fact that you're gonna get yourself killed."

"So what if I do? What are you, the Shadowman with a heart of gold? You're as bad as the Fehr. Scavengers. Murderers. I'm only helping 'cus you an' me got a common enemy."

He looked away from me. Blood coursed into his cheeks, coloring them with a rose tint.

"And what about her?" He pointed to the falling-down house in the distance, to where my mother waited in her bed for me to bring her dinner.

"What I said about my brother was true, you know."

I turned to look at the dark window, watching for her shadow to move inside. It didn't. She hardly ever moved without my help. "I can't keep her alive without him. Lincoln was special. She'd start bleeding somewhere and he could just look at her and make it stop. Even when it was on the inside and me and Dad didn't know what was wrong. He could just look at her and tell us right where she was broke and before too long she was fine again. Smiling again. Up and singing while she did the wash. But he's gone now. And she'll die."

I was telling the truth this time. No tears. No sniffling. Just my plain words.

"I'm sorry," he said. "Doesn't change the fact that your little expeditions are putting us both at risk."

"And what you are puts me at risk. I promise not to kill anybody. Not while my mom's still alive, anyway."

He rolled his eyes.

"I guess that's the best I'm gonna get."

I smiled.

"No. I've got something better for you."

He placed his hands on his hips and tilted his head forward, staring at me with his eyebrows drawn and his forehead all wrinkled up like before.

"The reason you're here. It's the woman, isn't it? The one whose face they keep plastering all over the skyboards every day." I pointed skyward, at the satellite-projected newscasts that lit up the sky. "The Red Lily."

"How did you…"

"She showed up right before you did. Just after winning some big battle against the Shadowmen. I put it together. Anyway, I know where you can find her."

I turned around and started walking back toward the house.

"Wait," he called after me. "Details."

"Later. I've gotta get Mom her dinner." I paused, looking back over my shoulder. "You don't look like a Shadowman, you know."

"I know. Half-breed."

"They do that?" I said, half to him and half to the empty desert as I walked toward my house.

"Some do," I heard him say from behind me.

"Huh."

CHAPTER 3

LEUKA FALKENER

I pulled a heavy crate off the back of the Ministry-issued utility vehicle and cringed. The pain shot through my broken ribs like lightning. I had wrapped them tight in bandages, but they still hurt like hell. Cece grabbed the crate from my arms, shaking her head at me.

The sun was high and still rising, reflecting off the white sand like a clean sheet of metal. Smooth and flat all the way out to the rippling dunes in the distance. Not a footprint, human or otherwise. "Someone remind me why I'm carting out rations to the middle of an empty desert?"

There wasn't a cloud in the pale blue sky. Would it have been too much to ask for a rainstorm?

"It's not empty," Cece said.

"Really? Because all I see is undisturbed sand and abandoned shanties."

Soldes shook his head. "They're not abandoned. They want it to look that way, so they'll be left alone. Ever heard of Shankers?"

I shivered at the word.

"They're for real? I thought that was just something my father told me when I was little to keep me from wandering off alone when we visited the capitol."

I scanned the horizon the way I would any battlefield. My flesh rose into goose bumps though it was approaching one hundred degrees and the sun was beaming down unencumbered. Natural shade didn't exist out here; there was hardly a plant and no geographical features tall enough to cast a shadow. At least that left no place for them to hide. Except behind the buildings. My eyes jumped from shadow to shadow, inventing shapes in the far away dark.

A cool hand fell on my shoulder. I wrenched it off me before looking, twisting until its owner was crouched and facing the ground. Cece. I released her with a gasp.

"I'm sorry," I said as she flopped onto her butt in the sand.

"Wow. Best not to startle the Lily," Soldes called to his men, laughing.

"I didn't think flowers had teeth," one of his men called back.

"Don't worry, my lady. They stay underground until dark. Very sensitive to the heat," Cece whispered to me as she got back to her feet. She brushed the sand off her skirt like nothing had happened and continued unloading pre-packed bags of food from the crate onto a folding table.

"Are they…people?"

"They're pathetic. People maybe, but surely not men," Cece answered.

Her eyes were sharp and glued to the back of the

captain's head.

"Not them. The Shankers," I whispered.

"Oh. I believe they were once. Desert dwellers like me."

She kept unloading, but I stood still, staring at her like a child listening to campfire stories.

"How did they get…well, how they are?"

A wisp of black hair escaped from her braid and blew across her forehead on the barely-there breeze. She brushed it away. Every move she made seemed so graceful. So natural. Like she was part of the desert itself. Then she looked at me and shrugged both shoulders.

"What makes a man into a monster?"

"My father used to say they had no eyes and great, black leather wings. That they eat anything to survive—people, animals, whatever crosses their path. And can take more pain than any human ever could. They just keep fighting. Limbs torn off, guts spilling out of their bellies, they'll just keep coming at you."

I watched her face, waiting for her to tell me it wasn't true. That it was all a ghost story invented to make children behave. But her face was unchanged. Her eyes never met mine. She just kept stacking rations, her mouth closed.

"Just stories though, probably," I said.

She didn't answer.

I shook the image out of my head and grabbed another food crate from the vehicle.

"Do you think anyone will come?"

The captain nodded. "They're starving out here. They won't have a choice."

"I hope you're right. I don't want my first operation for the Ministry to be a failure. Not that they were too impressed with the idea in the first place."

"It's a good idea, my Lily. They wanted you to make them like the Ministry. Feeding the starving is a good place to start," Cece reassured me.

We set up the rest of the food and the water coolers and waited. I had already sweated through my lightweight white cotton shirt and was marinating in it. The heat was starting to get to me.

"Do you want the water out, too, my Lily?" asked one of the guards whose name I hadn't bothered to learn.

"Do I want the water out? I don't know. Let's see, it's about a thousand degrees out and we're in the middle of the desert." I shrugged my shoulders, awaiting a response that never came. He just kept looking at me with empty eyes and his mouth half open.

"I've got an idea. If you're incapable of common sense, raise your hand." He didn't move. Until I moved him, using my telekinesis to jerk his hand up above his head. He watched his arm move against his will, eyes wide like he thought he was possessed.

"Good. Now, if your hand is raised, you don't get to talk for the rest of the day. That means you, Private," I said, nodding at him.

"But, I'm actually a corporal, Lily."

I smacked him on the forehead, not hard enough to hurt, just enough to make an audible snap.

"Bad! That was a test. And you failed, Private."

He opened his mouth. I raised my hand, ready to smack him again if necessary. But he sighed and closed his mouth. I smiled at him and nodded, the sarcasm practically seeping out of my pores with the gallons of sweat I was losing.

The desert still looked empty. No one was showing

up. Were they that ungrateful for all the Ministry had done for this backwards little sandpit of a planet?

I wiped the sweat from my brow bone. My hair was wet with it and sticking to my face. I pulled it up into a knot on my head and fastened it with a pin.

Then I could see them, coming from across the desert. They rode horses, camels, donkeys—whatever they had, I suspected. Some just walked. I wondered how they could raise animals out here that didn't die of starvation or thirst.

The closer they got, the more the glaring sun defined their features, their mean narrow faces, bony and weathered from hard living. They were all lean muscle and bone, wrapped in olive skin that could handle this desert sun far better than my own. I was already turning pink from the exposure. But thin and haggard as they were, their eyes were full of pride. I pulled up the light hood of my top and let my face fall into shadow.

No one spoke to me, not at first. But their stern expressions began to soften as they filled their bellies with water, meat and bread. I relaxed a little. They spoke amongst themselves, some of them. A little girl stood across from me. She had no food in her hands, but spoke into the ear of a tall dark man who crouched beside her. She was pointing at me, her narrow-eyed glare detracting from the sweetness of her freckled face and almond-shaped brown eyes.

I picked up a bag containing meat, a quarter loaf of sourdough bread, and some goat cheese and walked toward her.

"Eat something, child. This is a gift from the Ministry."

She snatched the paper bag out of my hands.

"I've survived this long without the Ministry, despite

the Ministry—I should say. Keep your table scraps, bitch."

She turned the bag over and emptied it into the sand at my feet.

"We are trying to help you survive. You are free to remain out here in the desert if you so choose. The Ministry is only trying to facilitate that freedom by providing you with necessary provisions."

She laughed, but it sounded more like the caw of a carrion bird. The others had stopped eating. All eyes were on the two of us.

"This wasn't a desert until they got here. They pumped all of our water to the city and made our farmers into their slave labor force."

"Tokino factory laborers are paid for their work and given accommodations for free. That's hardly slave labor, child. It is economic advancement."

She stepped forward now, despite the man beside her attempting to pull her back. Cece moved closer to me, her arm touching mine.

"Ten men and boys in one room with a cement floor and no beds? Sixteen-hour work days? One shit bucket in the corner? Yeah, you're *advancing* us into our graves."

I shook my head in disbelief. She was only a child. How could she know? But something stuck out in my head. Teeth—he shut down my request to see the factories. Could this be what he was hiding?

She picked up the chunk of sand-covered meat and threw it at my chest. "Take your leftovers and get gone!"

The others were getting restless now, too. They milled about behind the child like a disorganized army rallying behind their general. Bread fell from their hands to lie in the sand. Then a chunk of half-eaten yak meat struck me in the cheek. Bits of bread, cheese, and more meat followed, pelting me like a hail storm. I stopped them in mid-air without moving a muscle. This silenced them for a moment, as they watched the food float and then fall to ground.

But the show of my foreign abilities only seemed to anger them more. I couldn't hear individual words, just a storm of shouting voices. My guards moved swiftly between us, swords drawn.

"Sheathe your weapons!" I screamed the words so loud my throat ached as I watched one of them rushing that angry child with his blade. Cece grabbed Captain Soldes by his sword arm, trying to pull him back from the crowd. He threw his elbow back, knocking it into her chin. She dropped to the sand, unconscious.

They didn't listen to my protests, just kept moving. Although they called themselves my guard, they did not take orders from me. I wondered who they answered to, but the captain had already told me upon our first meeting. The Triad.

The one in front grasped a handful of the little girl's sandy brown hair and pulled. The man beside her caught her in his arms, thrusting his body in front of her. I wondered if he was her father. The guardsman wrenched the child's body free of his grip as three of the others came down on him, holding their blades to his neck.

CHAPTER 4

RAELON TOREK

"Rescind your disparaging comments about the Ministry and your life may be spared. Refuse and you will be made an example of."

"Death first!" She held her head high and offered him her neck boldly.

I struggled against the three guards holding me down. My teeth squeezed together so hard my jaw ached with the grimace. But my body moved swiftly and in a flash I held two of the guardsmen in my grasp. I pulled myself halfway up on one knee, crushing the one man's throat beneath my shin. The other struggled as I squeezed his neck in an iron grip.

The third guard had lost his balance and fallen backwards, but was now springing to his feet, sword drawn and pointed at my heart. The woman moved before I could begin to form a plan. A blur of shimmering white. A hooded angel, full of fury and vengeance, sweeping down from the heavens to teach the mortals a lesson.

She waved her wrist. The blade at the child's neck flew through the air, puncturing the side of one of the water coolers and sticking out of it at a right angle, the hilt still vibrating in the air.

She threw Libby out of the guard's reach and dove in front of the sword that was meant to pierce my chest. Her shoulders lifted sharply as she sucked in a deep breath. I couldn't tell if the sword had sliced clean through her or if she'd stopped it in time with her voodoo. I could only see its hilt, perfectly motionless in the silent desert heat. She was kneeling in front of me, also motionless. I jumped to my feet, my pulse pounding lightning quick against my temples.

The tiniest wound had appeared in the center of her chest. The blood beaded and ran in a streak down the white cloth of her shirt. Sword still floating there, it had just barely pierced her skin. Now it levitated as if brandished by some phantom. She shot her furious gaze at the guard who had stabbed her and he was cast backwards as if rammed by a large bull. He landed several yards away and lay still, crumpled in the sand.

I circled around in front of her, every move slow, deliberate. She hadn't moved yet, still crouched low and ready to keep fighting. No one else had moved either. Except the guard she had catapulted. They stood still as statues—their eyes wide and fixed on her, like mine were. I reached forward and took hold of the sword by its ornate golden hilt, its tip still in her chest. It didn't move, her relentless mind was fixed on defense and held it like it was mounted in stone. A warrior's instinct.

I reached forward and put my hand over hers. It was so small, half of mine. And cool against my hot skin. My skin was always hot. I wondered if hers was always cool to the touch. I eased her hand down toward her side.

"It's over."

I pulled the sword from the air, knelt before her on one knee, and presented it to her with the blade lying across my palms. I was shocked to see her guards follow my lead and kneel before her, heads bowed. The rest of the desert dwellers, one by one, followed suit, kneeling as I had.

She took the sword from my hands, holding it with the slightest grip, as if it disgusted her. As I rose to my feet, I realized I was a full foot taller than her. Just a little girl, but she had fought like…well, like I would have. And her eyes were so deep and green I could not look away from them. I had never seen eyes so furious and proud. I should have said something.

Say something, I kept telling myself but there were no words in my mind. Only those eyes.

I swallowed hard and opened my mouth but then closed it again. I nodded my head, but never lowered my eyes from hers. Then the captain of her guard was behind her, placing his hand on her shoulder. I didn't like watching him touch her. That was stupid, but it's what I felt. I was there to stalk and kill her, to take my revenge for her humiliating me in battle. But if the man didn't walk away soon, I might rip his arm off and beat him to death with it.

"We must go, my lady. The Ministry will want an explanation," her handmaiden urged her.

"Yeah, okay."

She turned away from me and back to her men. One of them gathered up the imbecile who had stabbed her from where he lay on the ground and tossed him into the back of her vehicle. Unconscious but still breathing.

She sat beside him in the back, her fingers on his neck, probably checking his pulse. If it was me, I would have thrown him in the desert and left him for the Shankers.

I didn't take my eyes off her as they drove away. Her hands, her sunburned legs, her fingers on the neck of the broken fool beside her. Dammit. Why had she done that? Why had she saved me?

CHAPTER 5

LEUKA FALKENER

I paced back and forth so long I thought I'd worn a trail in the creaky wood of my outside deck. It looked out over the water. A pretty view. But I hadn't glanced up since we got back. I stared at my own two hands, each fiddling with the fingers of the other as I walked.

My skin hummed with energy. It was like I could feel every individual cell. And they were eager. Anxious. That scene in the desert felt like a battle. But no blood had been spilled, with the exception of the tiny bead of my own that had trickled down and dried on my chest. No battle stations to be manned or troops to command. No check. No mate.

Something in me felt cheated. Not my mind. My mind was thanking fate that no lives had been lost, no more numbers added to my body count. But physically, my body had prepared for a war. All that tension with no release had my blood boiling under my skin.

I didn't bother to look up and see the sun sinking on the horizon, but my shadow was pale, stretched out long and thin, the way it did when day met night.

I had to do something. I had to act. To move and sweat and work until my muscles ached and my mouth was dry and panting. Until my body was too exhausted to let my mind stay awake any longer.

I glanced out over the reservoir once before sprinting down the narrow steps and running toward the desert. They were at my heels before I even rounded the corner of my house. Like dogs. Except I liked dogs.

"Where are you going at this hour, my Lily?"

I didn't stop at his voice. Captain Soldes would have to sprint if he wanted to talk to me.

"For a run," I said between breaths.

"It's nearly dark, Lily."

"Nearly. But not quite," I said.

"We should get you back to the estate," he said, clearly becoming short of breath.

I stopped and turned to him.

"Soldes. I am *going* for a run. You and your boys can follow along like good puppies or go back by yourselves. But you and I both know you're not going to take me back if I don't want to go. You're not fast enough, and frankly, I don't think you're bold enough."

His head sank at this, eyes falling to the sand. I was right and he knew it.

"So if you're coming along, keep the chatter to a minimum. I'll be doing my best to pretend you don't exist."

I took off again. I heard their breathing and my own, their footfalls and my own, and the gentle whoosh of the sand as our feet skimmed through it. I pushed hard until the estate was the size of my little finger in the distance and the moon was fat and round and low, but rising in the corn blue sky. Then I slowed to a jog and bent forward, holding my thighs in my hands and letting my breath slow down.

The sound I heard was pretty, at first. A whistle, like the air singing as it slid over the metal wing of a sleek spacecraft. By the time I looked up to identify its source, Soldes was dead.

The thing on his body was charcoal black. All I saw at first were the wings. Angled like an osprey, leathery like a bat. It was hunched over him. I couldn't see what it was doing, but I heard something ripping. And voices screaming. Some of the others had run. Some of them were nearby, hunched over and gagging and spilling the contents of their stomachs into the sand.

The creature whirled around to face me. I felt the air wash over me as it spun, the splash of thick warm blood against my face. I was standing still. Perfectly still. Unable to move, to think, to react.

The monster charged me, wings outstretched like a horror from a nightmare. I pushed, my arms out, directing my telekinesis at its chest. It slowed, but kept coming, step by step. Its eyeless face was splattered with Soldes's blood.

I clenched my jaw and pushed forward. It felt like pushing my hands against a brick wall. My body might move backward before the beast in front of me was stopped. Teeth bared, it pressed toward me.

It would not be stopped. I waited, letting it push against my will and inch closer until it was feet from reaching me with its clawed fingertips. Then I let go, all at once, dropping to the sand as I did and somersaulting under its wing. The creature burst forward when I dropped my arms, running past me.

I jumped to my feet to run, but something tripped me. I was caught up in it like a rope or tubing. But it was wet and warm and when I looked down I found that it was Soldes, his intestines torn out and tangled around me. I dropped to my knees and vomited.

Hands wrapped around my wrists. It was another of my guards. I hadn't bothered to learn his name. He pulled me to my feet, pulled hard until my ankles slipped free of their bloody fetters and I could run. The others, those of them who hadn't run, were circling the eyeless creature with their swords drawn.

The creature sniffed the air through slits of nostrils, moving its head from side to side as it did. Then it cocked its head back and opened its wide jaws. The sound that came out was something like a scream, but deeper, raspier. It was the most terrifying sound I'd ever heard. Until the others called back. Then it was a chorus of raspy screams. It seemed to come from all around me, the way it echoed in the empty desert. When I turned, I saw them approaching, three of them, in the distance but closing fast and each coming from a different direction.

The one that killed Soldes was swatting away sword strokes like they were mosquitoes. One of them got lucky and sliced right through that leather skin and deep in the thing's chest.

"Die, scum," he yelled. But the creature didn't stop for a second. It clutched the guard's sword arm and pulled him forward, forcing the sword in deeper until the blade stuck out of its back and the hilt was pressed firmly against its charcoal skin. Then it leaned in hard and sank its jagged teeth into the man's throat. It was so fast I didn't have time to look away. It yanked its head back, ripping out the front my guard's throat.

We were all going to die here.

I dropped back to the sand, paralyzed by my helplessness, my fear.

No. I wouldn't die here. And neither would anyone else. The beast was too strong for me to move. My men were not, as I'd learned earlier in the desert. I thrust my arms out toward them and they slid across the sand until they were a safe distance from our attacker. Behind him.

I glanced over my shoulder. The other three monsters were still out of reach, but closing fast. This was my window and it wouldn't last long. I raised my hands skyward and the sand followed. It floated up over my head. Hundreds of pounds of it. I might not be able to move the Shanker, but sand was easy. It had no will of its own to fight with mine. I pushed until my body shook like a skeleton in a hurricane. The sand gathered in a cloud above its head. I released it. And ran.

I didn't look back until I reached the guards. What was left of them, anyway. They ran alongside me back toward the estate. Over my shoulder, I saw the Shanker's wings poking out of the sand, writhing in the struggle to unearth itself from its tomb. The others had reached it. They didn't stop to help it. Just bolted past it and toward their prey. Toward us.

I paused for just a second, glaring at them, though they couldn't see my face. Expression helped sometimes. Jaw set, eyes narrowed. It communicated my intent to my brain. Also I was pissed. I clapped my hands together overhead and sent a tidal wave of sand rolling toward them. It picked up speed with every inch, barreling into the beastly onslaught and burying them. I didn't wait.

Didn't watch to see if they would get back up. They would. They'd wriggle and writhe themselves free of the sand and keep coming for blood. We could only run.

And run we did.

The men could barely keep up with me. Fear kept me moving fast. I wouldn't leave them behind. But unless one of them dropped, I wasn't slowing down. By the time we reached the estate I was soaked through with cold sweat and panting like a dog. I didn't stop to catch my breath until we were all through the door.

The men who had fled were inside already. They were sitting on the floor, looking more like middle schoolers around a campfire than Ministry-trained guards, ghost stories on their faces. Their heads snapped up when I slammed the door behind me. I bolted it shut. I slid the chain lock into place, but it didn't seem like enough. They'd been so strong.

My eyes went to the sofa. Plain, but sturdy. Solid wood frame. I no more than blinked and it shot across the living room floor, flipping up on one side as it reached the door.

"Lily, it's all right. You're safe, now," the guard next to me said. He was still panting from our run and sweat had soaked his short black hair so it stuck in bits to his forehead.

"Yeah. Tell that to Soldes," I said, still searching the room for heavy pieces of furniture.

"We could if you hadn't gotten him killed." The voice came from below. The guard who had spoken was sitting cross-legged on my floor with his big eyes wide and his thick squat hands running over his shaved head again and again.

I ignored him, but the man beside me didn't.

"Yeah, Miller? The rest of us would be dead, too, if she hadn't been there. Where were you? Oh, right. You bolted to save your own ass."

Miller stood.

"You calling me a coward?" he said, inching forward as he did, his chest puffed up like a gorilla in mating season.

"Was I not clear enough about that? I'm sorry. Not only are you a coward, you are a slimy, self-serving, deserter bitch."

"Say that one more time and you'll wish she let the Shankers have you."

"Enough," I cried and the two men flew backward, as if propelled by my voice, until their backs struck opposing walls. "What's your name?" I said to my defender.

"Barvai Dushuku, my Lily." He nodded his head as he spoke to me.

"Congratulations, Barvai. You've been promoted to captain." I started to walk away, until his voice stopped me.

"Ma'am, that's not exactly how it works."

"It is now," I said. The two other men sitting on the carpet stood, protest in their eyes, mouths open and full of fire just waiting to burst forth. I didn't even look at them this time. They just shot backwards until they were pinned against the wall, too.

"If anyone has call to question my authority on this matter. . . let's just say I wouldn't advise it."

I turned around and faked a big yawn as I strode to my bedroom, though my eyes were wide open and would likely stay that way until the sun rose high and chased away the shadows. There would be no restful slumber for me tonight. Tonight, monsters were real.

CHAPTER 6

LIBERTY RHODE

I ran. Bare feet pounding the sand, kicking up little bursts of it that scratched at my ankles. It was hot. Burning hot. Like running through tar. But I couldn't care about that right now.

The sun was sinking low on the horizon, so low I thought it might never rise again. I didn't want to stop. But my legs were wobbling, and sucking in another ragged breath seemed impossible. It would explode in my chest and take the whole desert with me. I only meant to pause for a second. Let my breath slow down until I could run again, but the second my feet were still, my knees buckled and I was in the sand. That low orange sun cast its glow over my blood-covered body. There was so much. Soaking my shirt, painting my hands and arms. The sand stuck to it. I tried to brush it off and it burned. I didn't know I was screaming until Raelon was there, covering my mouth with his hand.

"Shhhhhh."

He was on his knees in front of me. When the screaming stopped, he let his hand fall down.

"So much blood," I whispered.

"What did you do?"

I didn't understand.

"Do? What did I do?" I repeated like a bad recording.

"Dammit, Lib. You said you wouldn't kill anyone."

"Oh," was all I could respond as I realized what he was saying. I looked back toward the house.

"I didn't kill her. Didn't save her either." Tears came now. Real tears. It'd been years since I'd let myself cry real tears. Now I thought they might never stop. They might flow on forever until the desert was fertile again and the crops started growing, 'til the starving folks out here were full-bellied and free and smiling.

"Your mother?"

I nodded.

Then his two big arms wrapped around me, pulling me to his chest and rocking me back and forth. My eyes fell closed. There was only warm skin against mine and the soothing sway of our bodies.

Then he let go. So fast I dropped onto my butt in the sand. He was staring at his hands like he didn't recognize them. Like he'd just touched something foul and was making sure it didn't stick.

"I have to leave, kid. I'm sorry."

"Now?"

He didn't look at me. Didn't speak. Just nodded his head, climbing back up to his feet.

"So that's it. I got no one left," I said.

I couldn't look at him, felt my eyes stinging. It was enough that he'd seen me crying like a cranky infant. I wouldn't let it happen again.

"I'm truly sorry you lost your mother."

"Yeah, well I don't need a shoulder to cry on and sorry don't spill no blood."

He reached forward like he might touch my face, but pulled his hand back before it made contact.

"I'm a Shadowman. And I came here for a reason."

"The Lily? You're still going after her?"

I shook my head and let the anger fill up the empty space I'd forced my sorrow to vacate.

"Why wouldn't I?"

"She saved my life. She saved your life."

He looked over his shoulder, running his hand through his careless dark hair. "This is bigger than you, Lib. It's too big for you to understand right now."

"No. I think it's bigger than *you* understand. You talk like you're different than the other Shadowmen, like you're better. But you're not. You're just a coward."

I spit on the sand in front of his feet.

"Go on then," I shouted.

He stood still and shrugged.

"I could wait 'til the morning…"

"Get off my property, coward. And don't come back for that piece of space-waste in my barn either. I'll probably sell it for scrap."

"Libby."

I punched him in the stomach as hard as I could manage. He could have blocked it but didn't.

"Don't call me that. Just go!"

He turned his back and took a few steps before looking over his shoulder.

"Be safe, Liberty," he said.

"I'm not safe. Ain't nobody here safe and we ain't

gonna be until somebody rises up. And you're about to hunt down and kill the best hope we've seen."

He took three angry strides back toward me.

"She's Ministry, Libby! She's the enemy! That stunt in the desert, that was publicity. She's manipulating you and I bet the whole damn Ministry Council helped to plan it."

I stared at him hard, my eyes boring into his and daring him to look away. "You're wrong." I shook my head, sighing. "Just go, Raelon. You're pointless."

I didn't wait for him to go this time, just turned my back and started walking. The blood on my hands had dried. The sun had set. And the place I knew as home was just an ugly wooden tomb. I didn't hear footsteps behind me, but there was no point looking back. Whether he was still standing there or not, Raelon was gone.

CHAPTER 7

RAELON TOREK

I was squeezed tight in the crawl space tucked between the basement and the western half of the house, floorboards above me, cool packed dirt beneath me. The eastern side of the house appeared to be an addition. It was shiny and new with a full basement dug out of the sand. The western half was probably the original house, with worn out wood that creaked and bowed every time it was stepped on.

I was safe here. Safe and alone. Concealed in the shadows and able to move about beneath the house at will. There was one way in and one way out, a small opening next to the basement stairs. It was the only place I might be vulnerable. But that was a risk I had to take.

I'd been on this planet too long, doing too many things that were not my mission. Staying with the kid had been a mistake. Even so, I kept picturing her—that freckled little face soaked in tears, body sunk down to her knees, all covered in blood and sand. Some little piece of stranger inside me wanted to go back. But that's not who I was. I was a warrior. A killer.

Through the floorboards the shadows of her delicate bare feet danced above me as she padded around her bedroom. The other rooms in the house had solid flooring, updated recently. Interesting she'd chosen the oldest room, the one with dusty, cracked floorboards and no insulation, as her bedroom.

I was blind in the other rooms, but moved with her anyway, listening to the way the floor creaked as she walked. She spent a lot of time in the basement and outside on the beach training. A few hours every morning. Through dirty basement windows I watched her, pink and sweaty and bathed in morning sunlight.

I couldn't get close enough to her to finish it. Her guards were within a few feet of her at all times. Even when she slept. I'd been stuck here for weeks, eating dehydrated meat from my pockets to survive. The black hours gave me enough cover to crawl out through the ground-level basement window and gather provisions, relieve myself, stretch. Then it was back to the hole.

She was as frustrated with her twenty-four-hour supervision as I was. Her windows were barred and she spent a lot of time shut in her bedroom, but even there she was not alone. They posted a guard at her bedside as she slept. They moved outside the door, leaving it slightly ajar when she dressed in the morning. Same routine when she bathed herself. She sang like a caged bird while she washed. I'd never heard a Fehr man or woman sing like that—especially a military commander. Music and art weren't encouraged among the Fehr. Too provocative.

Today she sang, voice echoing over the running water,

sweet and pure. She must have heard the song on a colony planet. My fingers started to move, drumming against the wooden floorboards to the cadence of her song. I was lost in her melody. Until she paused, my tapping the only noise. I balled my hands up into fists and held them at my side. Careless. I could have revealed myself. It was hard, being alone for so long. I hadn't spoken to another person since Libby. Sometimes I whispered to myself in the dark, just to break up the silence.

After a few long seconds, she continued. I lay beneath her bathroom and listened to the pouring water as she showered. Her voice cut through the silence in this dark, dusty hole. Then a soft whine, the handle turning. The water stopped running.

A soft male voice, "My lady?"

Then a storm of shattering glass. My pulse pounded up into my temples. I listened, holding my breath and waiting to hear her voice.

"Captain, if I ever see your eyes on my body again, I will rip them out of their orbits without getting my hands dirty! Now get out," she yelled.

I smiled, biting back the laugh that was itching in the back of my throat. I had never heard a Fehr woman yell like that. They were so cool and passionless. But not this one.

The door slammed.

"What in the hell could he need so desperately that he had to interrupt me while I'm bathing?"

She was talking to herself now. She did that a lot.

"Isn't it obvious what he needed?" I whispered my response out loud and it felt good to talk to another person, even if she couldn't hear me. "He needed to see you undressed and dripping from the tub."

I crept along the floor beneath her as her footsteps led me down the hall and into her room.

"You," she snapped. "Go clean up the glass. I will be in my bedroom dressing myself. If any of you would like to bleed to death from empty eye sockets, please, interrupt me while I'm naked."

I held my breath to keep from laughing out loud. She was so unusual. Although she had proven that weeks ago when she'd nearly taken a sword through the heart to save my life. Libby said she was different. Naïve child, she saw only the crystal surface of the lake, not the miles of polluted slime underneath.

She'd had no logical reason to save me, to fight her own guards, but she had anyway. Her actions had turned her into a heroic figure to the desert dwellers. It was a stunt for the Ministry. Publicity. And it had worked. The peasants hadn't stopped talking about her, painting portraits to each other with their dramatic descriptions of her, standing in front of Libby, shielding her with her own body. The story had spread like a virus, with help from the Ministry. Every media projection lighting up the skyboards overhead glowed with her image. It was a brilliant strategy. Cunning and deceitful.

Her door creaked closed and I shifted beneath her until I was under her bedroom. Her outline silhouetted by the fading light from the window behind her and down through the gaps in the weathered old floorboards to my lonely eyes. She dropped her towel to the floor and pulled some garment from the closet. No wonder the guards couldn't keep their eyes to themselves. The curve of her body, even just its outline, was something remarkable. She was a landscape painted by a master. A wilderness skyline, untamed and untamable.

She pulled on the backless dress and it draped over her form like it was fluid. The halter neckline wrapped around her neck and fed into an oversized hood. She often wore hoods, probably to protect her delicate Fehr eyes from the sun. As she pulled the hood up, the pale skin of her back was exposed down to the dimples just above the curve of her buttocks. I blinked and looked away. I'd been alone in this hole for too damn long. Focus, I told myself. I turned back to see her bent toward her ankle sliding shoes onto her feet.

She held up one hand and the black screws twisted out from the bars on her windows. When the screws were out, they floated, the bars following them, as if all the gravity had been sucked out of the room. They moved slow, landing on her bed without compressing a single coil on the spring mattress. It was so dead silent that if my eyes had been closed, I would have thought the room empty.

But I didn't dare close my eyes. It was like watching a magic show, and I was unable to blink for fear that I might miss the performer revealing his trick. But there was no trick. She was just that good. Palm pressed flat on the window sill, she hopped out, her entire body compressing into a tight crouch in mid-air to fit through.

There was no pause, not even the space of a breath between the moment she vanished through the window and the moment I pursued her. My belly dragged against the dirt floor as I crawled on knees and forearms toward the opening, spilling out onto the basement stairs and sprinting to the window. I had to be fast; the guards would be looking for her soon and the moon would not set for hours.

I popped the dirty basement window open and threw

myself out, sprawling onto the sand, limbs tied up. Clumsy. My mind was fevered, body possessed with my single-minded pursuit.

Gone. By the time I rose, it was as if she'd never been there. But there was no cover in this desert lawn of hers. She had taken to the water. It was the only way she could escape without being seen or leaving a trail.

The sky grew darker by the minute, but the moon still reflected a silvery glow across the face of the reservoir. She was swimming across, heading for the Dega ports. It was miles away, an impressive swim. But I had watched her train every day. She could handle it.

Swimming after her was not an option. If she didn't see me, her guards would and I'd lead them straight to her. I couldn't take the beach road either. That would be the first place they hunted for her. The rocky cliff face loomed black and jagged to my left. It was the shortest distance, provided the best cover. The cliff face was slippery, its glassy black rock misted by the great body of water beneath it. It jutted out of the water, every crack and shadow reaching up for the moon overhead. It wouldn't be easy. But I always did enjoy a challenge.

I held my breath and ran into the cool water. Aiming for the spot across from me where the white waves rolled, foamy and soft, into the black rock, I dove beneath them and swam underwater until my chest burned from holding the air inside. Then I swam farther.

It was dark under the water with my eyes closed tight. Dark and calm and cool against my raging mind. When my head felt light enough to float away, when the back of my neck felt hot and tingly despite the cool water and I thought I might have forgotten which way the surface was and which way was deep abyss, I finally came up. One deep breath. I opened my eyes for just a second to judge my distance from the cliff, then dove back beneath the water, pushing ever forward, carried by my compulsion.

I reached the rocky shore and hauled my chest up out of the water, heavy and soaking wet. My hands were slippery. It was hard to get a grip on the jutting rocks, to find footholds to cling to as the waves rose and fell, rocking me up and down in their hypnotic embrace. I started slow. The jagged edges dug into my palms. My foot slipped as I eased my lower body up out of the water, slamming into the unforgiving rock, but I corrected fast and accurate. I climbed until the misty spatter from below no longer reached me, and then climbed faster. Soon I was speeding up the cliff, pulling my body up with my arms as I leapt through the night sky from foothold to foothold.

From the top, every ripple in the water sparkled in silver moonlight. It was so beautiful I had to make myself look away. She wasn't there. But my instincts told me she hadn't reached the shore yet. Maybe she was swimming underwater to hide her presence. Or maybe she'd drowned. No. She was alive. I knew it, just like in combat when I knew an enemy was about to strike. I could feel it in my blood and bones.

So I ran. My skin on fire. No mission had felt so desperate. Every cell in my body was aching to close the space between us. I could catch her as she crawled out onto the beach. Maybe. I ignored my pounding heartbeat, my burning chest begging me to stop and catch my breath. I blocked it all out. There was only the sound of my feet hitting the sandy ground.

CHAPTER 8

LEUKA FALKENER

Logically I knew there was no one behind me. The guards could not have caught up with me yet. They were well trained, but also dull witted and lacking motivation. I looked around the beach, peered beneath the docks, and saw no one. But I felt someone. I felt like I was being watched. Hunted.

It was unreasonable to get spooked by a feeling. Feelings, by their nature, are unreasonable. There was no evidence, no proof, I reminded myself. I looked around one more time before sprinting off in the direction of the aeronautics factory in Dega South. There was nothing special about this factory that separated it from the rest. But it was the closest, hanging on the outer edge of the industrial district. The easiest to sneak inside.

My guardsmen had forbidden me from coming to Dega South. They said it was rampant with crime and too dangerous for a woman like me. But they'd never known a woman like me. And what I'd come here for was more dangerous than anything creeping in back alleys or hiding behind dumpsters. Knowledge.

Hood pulled up around my face, I tried to keep to the shadows. But those few that I passed didn't want to be seen any more than I did. Half-starved men followed scantily-clad women into falling down buildings. Cash traded hands for vials of green and red liquid, the synthetic drugs that had become so popular in this part of the city.

At first glance, the factory looked benign. Just a tall drab building with few windows. It was the color of smoke, narrow and looming overhead like a great chimney. Then I saw the guards. They hid in towers high above the entrances and exits, holding long, scoped firearms. These cheap, clumsy weapons had been banned for decades, yet here they were, in the arms of the black-clad figures guarding a Ministry-sanctioned factory.

Something about the gun held me there, stone still and gaping like a stunned child, when I should be running for cover. The gleam of the black metal in the moonlight. It looked so heavy. I imagined the weight of it in my arms. The long barrel seemed to shorten as it was turned to face me. Only then did I look up to the man wielding it, the black lenses of his perfectly round goggles trained on me.

The shot rang out and all I had time to think about was how loud it was. Ear splitting. I held up one hand, flinching away from the flash of the barrel and waiting. I waited too long for such a weapon. For the blood, the pain. It didn't come. When I looked up again the bullet was hanging in the air, inches from my outstretched hand. I snatched it out of the air. Still hot, it rolled over the lines in my palm until I dropped it to the pavement. These weren't pacifying rounds. They were tiny missiles, violent and personal. He'd aimed for a kill shot.

It took him a moment to realize I hadn't taken his bullet. His aim had been true and I had made no attempt to move from its deadly path. But awareness must have set in. He was lining up another shot.

I could have run, had all the time I needed to dive behind the corner of the building and take cover. The barrel was just a tiny black circle from this angle, pointed straight at me. I only narrowed my eyes. No plan. No thought in my head. Just fury. The black-clad figure launched from his little crow's nest before he could fire. For a moment, I only watched. He flailed his limbs, grasping at the air itself as he came crashing down.

I'd done that. I realized almost too late. He stopped at the very last second, his mask-covered face an inch from kissing the pavement. I let him fall that last inch and sprinted over. My white bone knife was at his throat like a ghost in the night, my other arm hooked around his neck. He panted like a dog, hot breath moist on my arm. It made me gag, being this close to him. Like he was contagious. I pushed him forward and away from me. He started to run.

"I could have killed you before, you know? All the way up on that tower. What do you think I could do from this close?"

He stopped, back to me, raising both hands in the air.

"Do what I say and you get to keep your intestines on the inside."

He nodded, still not looking back.

"Good. Now walk."

I took him into a shadowy alley beside the dumpster.

We were out of view of the other marksmen here.

"Why did you try to kill me?"

He stared at me, frozen. The fury in my eyes reflected back at me in his dark goggles, my face distorted by their perfect round lenses. I sighed, reached forward and pulled his mask and goggles off in one motion. He looked no more than eighteen, his brown mop of hair tousled from the mask I'd yanked off his head.

"Speak."

"Orders. No one in or out without authorization. Shoot to kill."

"Orders from whom?"

"The Triad. Stone Fist himself gave us the kill order."

"Why does the Triad want to keep people out of the factories?"

"You're the first person we've had to keep out."

I just looked at him. The question must have been apparent on my face, because he spoke again.

"The guns are to keep them in. If they try to escape, we make an example of them."

I shook my head back and forth, back and forth until the alley started to blur. I'd believed in them. Fought for them. Killed for them.

I was on the wrong side.

"Does the Minister know of this?"

He held up his hands, shrugged his shoulders. "I'm just Ministry Guard. All I know is that we get orders from the Triad. They know everything that goes on here. They control it."

I picked up his gun and pointed it between his eyes.

"Give me your clothes."

He didn't hesitate to strip naked and lay his garments at my feet. Too bad these things were illegal. I loved the intimidation factor. No one underestimated a little girl with a big gun. Telekinesis was more effective, but couldn't be brandished in the same way.

"Get in the dumpster."

He climbed into the stinking metal container, shivering as I slammed the lid and slid a heavy iron bar through the holes to seal it. It would be easy to escape. I looked at it for another second, considering, then held up both hands and focused my intent. The thick steel bar twisted like a pretzel. That would hold him.

I pulled on his black coveralls and zipped it up over my clothes. The mask felt suffocating, but I yanked it down over my face anyway and stuck on the shiny round goggles. Through their gleaming lenses the night was tinted green, the darkness lifted away. I could see every creature, moving through the shadow, from the crows pecking for scraps along the roadside to the black-clad guards marching along the perimeter of the building. I rushed to the perch from which I'd thrown my would-be killer, gun slung over my back, and climbed the spiraling metal stairs, stumbling in my haste.

From the top I could see into every corner of the tall narrow building. I aimed the gun inside, using the scope to spy through the sparse windows. The workers were barefoot. Their ribs poking out of their pale, bruised flesh. They worked fast, fumbling parts together with their bare sweaty hands. When they dropped bits of metal, someone struck them in the back with a heavy rope two or three times, tearing their clothes, bruising if not breaking their skin. They didn't dare drop to their knees; that only seemed to spur on the rage of their tormentors.

The clanging ring of feet falling on metal pulled

my gaze from the factory to the spiral stairs beneath me. Others, dressed like the poor fool I had left in the dumpster, ran up the tower steps with guns in tow. Only one way down.

I had never attempted using telekinesis to move my own body. I knew it was an advanced skill that few had mastered, but at the moment I had no other option. I leapt over the railing of the tower, trying to focus my racing mind. The ground rushed toward me too fast. Don't panic, I told myself as the glistening black pavement grew closer and closer. I closed my eyes. My fall began to slow. I hit the ground, landing hard on my butt and left thigh, but slow enough that I didn't hear bones snapping from within me. I'd have to work on that.

Their guns were aimed my way as I hopped to my feet. I ripped them from their hands before they could pull a single trigger and sent them flying like shrapnel in a firefight.

My fury carried me. I was at the big metal doors before the sentries could get to their feet. It was barred from the outside. Not wood. The bar was iron and damn heavy. But I only had to glance at it, and it flew like a toothpick in a hurricane.

The sentries had risen now, and were sprinting toward me. A pack of them. I jutted my arms forward and felt the power in the movement, like my own two arms could have stopped a speeding train. The iron bar flew, striking them across their midsections. The whole pack crumpled to the ground. Some of them stirred, but most of them were still.

The doors flew open at my will and I stormed inside. The men with ropes in their hands looked at me, dumbfounded. The workers stared in fear, like it was the only emotion they remembered how to feel.

It was worse from inside—one huge factory floor, no air flow, bars on the windows. The heat struck me at the same time as the smell, with more force than a brick to the temple. It was thick, that smell. Almost visible, the stench of human waste wafting from dirty white buckets at the end of each assembly line. But it mixed in the air with the metal and fuel, the sweat and blood. The stone floor was painted with it. Dry dark stains and new wet puddles stretched out across the room like islands on a map.

The workers stared at me. Their eyes were sunken and dull. Most of them did not stop their work when they saw me burst through the doors. One of them paused, looking at me curiously, some shiny interlocking gears still clutched in his skeletal hand. The enforcer heaved his rope and struck it across his back so hard he buckled to his knees. It was thicker than my upper arm and stained an ugly red-brown.

I counted thirty of them, swinging their ropes around and walking taller than the rest. Fools. Weak men given their first taste of what they thought was power.

He struck the man again and this time his legs buckled and he fell to his knees. My eyes popped wide open and angry. Every window shattered inward and rained broken glass over us like the ash that falls from the heavens when a volcano erupts. I wasn't sure that I had caused it at first. It didn't feel like my normal telekinesis. It was like a shockwave of fury pulsing out of my guts and through my skin, vibrating the floor and walls of the building until the glass gave way.

I marched to the closest enforcer. He was still crouched and shielding his head from the shower of glass. I yanked the mask from his face.

He came up swinging that damn rope. It cracked like a whip snapping toward me. But it stopped, changing course in mid-air and winding itself around his body from the tips of his toes to his thick tan neck. I nodded. The rope pulled him up until his toes wiggled back and forth, searching for a bit of solid ground to stand on.

"You beat and starve and kill your own people. And for what? Power?"

I dropped him, letting him writhe around on the floor, desperate to free himself of the bloody rope. The others were coming, taking tentative steps toward me. The dumb curiosity on their faces replaced by simple fear. Good. They should fear me.

They circled around until I was surrounded, smacking those thick bloody ropes against their palms. "You think swinging a rope gives you power? I'll show you power."

It hurt, at first. The surge of energy threw me forward and I fell to one knee, crouching. When I snapped my head up, all thirty of them shot high into the air, their ropes falling raggedly to the stone below. The workers howled like wild animals, hungry for the blood of their captors. I shared their hunger. Blind with rage I thrust the men higher above us, dangling them like a chandelier, much to the pleasure of my audience.

I smiled as I flung their twitching frantic bodies out the windows and listened to them scream. The workers cheered at the bloodshed. Except for one, just a few feet in front of me. He was a child, probably ten years old. His face was so dirty that the whites of his eyes showed like two glowing stars surrounding the deep brown iris and dilated pupil. He shivered, staring at my smiling face, and I realized he was afraid. Of me. And he should be.

I pulled hard with every muscle and fiber and cell in my body and slowed the falling men. I could feel them. They hit the ground hard but would survive. I hoped.

What was happening to me? A few minutes ago I had struggled to control the speed of my own falling body, and now I did the same thing with thirty men that I couldn't even see.

I stepped toward the quivering boy in front of me, reaching for him but he recoiled. I pulled the mask and goggles off of my face in one motion and dropped to my knees in front of him. "It's okay, child. I won't hurt you."

As the mask fell at my feet, so did the workers. Each of them lay their dirty foreheads to the stone, bowing to me as I knelt in front of them. Not a Fehr bow. Their own gesture of respect. I stood. There were hundreds of them. An army. This was the uprising the Ministry had feared. And I was the spark that had lit the inferno.

I raised both my hands. It took all my energy just to lift the weight of them after all the energy I had exerted. I motioned toward the door. "You are free, now. Leave this prison."

CHAPTER 9

RAELON TOREK

This was it. She ran from the factory alone. Every inch of her dove-white skin was enveloped in the oversized uniform. But I knew it was her from the way she moved. Deliberate. Graceful. She flew through the gleaming black city streets, never stepping in a puddle or tripping on an uneven stone in the sidewalk, though she didn't once look down.

She had fought her own kind again, freed the slave laborers. Had Libby been right about her? Of course she had; that perceptive little pain in the ass could read people like I had never seen. She *was* different. But did it matter? I wasn't here to fight the war of another people. I was here to kill the woman so I could go back home.

Half-shadow. I could still hear the Alpha's voice spitting the words at me. Sympathy is what he would expect from me. I was not weak. This was not my war.

She stopped in a narrow alley. Caught off guard, my

heart raced so hard I could feel the blood bounding through the arteries in my neck with its every beat. I dropped to my knees and crawled over to the ditch, the cool water seeping through the knees of my pantlegs, which had only just dried from the swim. The ditch was half full of water, but I slid in anyway. There I lay in wait, my body submerged, all but my eyes and the top of my head.

She stripped off the disguise. She was facing my direction, head turning back and forth across the alley. Had she seen me? I was frozen still, a stone statue, a corpse in a coffin. *Don't breathe,* I told myself. *Don't blink.*

She turned back around and ran again. I struggled to keep up with her while staying just out of view. We ran past the Capitol, into Ministry Memorial gardens. Why here? She was too smart for this. There was no help for her out here. No safety. It would be too easy. I wanted to shake her by her shoulders until she snapped out of whatever fog she was in and started acting like the woman I knew. The one who was capable and brave and sharp as the bone blades she carried tucked into a belt around her thigh.

But that was absurd, wasn't it? I wanted her to protect herself from me? I couldn't explain it, even in my own head. I just knew the anger I felt burning under my skin. Anger that I knew her as someone so strong and worthy, and yet she was acting so weak and careless. Like I'd been fooled.

She slowed down now to a brisk walk. Her gray dress clung to her body, soaking wet and heavy. Masses of limp, wet, strawberry hair hung across her forehead and in her eyes. She wiped at them with shaky fingers.

We passed through the gate to the military graveyard, she first but I wasn't far behind. I didn't understand. This wasn't logical, and logic was the Fehr compass. They lived and died by it. I ducked around the gate and crouched low with my back to a statue of a looming winged figure.

She had stopped. My back was to her, in my hiding place, but I heard her body still as her feet squished down in the soggy ground. I pulled my sword from its sheath and it felt heavier than it ever had. She's just a pawn, I told myself. But I didn't believe me.

I tried not to picture her in the desert, standing between me and her own guard's sword as it flew at her chest. She hadn't flinched. Even as the tip of that blade pierced her perfect skin. I had never seen her flinch.

I approached from behind her. She was kneeling now. I expected her to turn to me. Her senses were keen, reflexes too sharp. She should have heard me. But her body was shaking. I didn't understand at first. What were the noises coming from her? Was she ill? As I stepped closer, I realized. She was crying. Sobbing, actually. Her chest heaved as she panted, struggling for every breath through her tears, her nose pouring snot down her face.

This was the last thing I had expected. I had never seen this raw emotion in any Fehr man or woman. What was she? As I circled around to her flank, I saw the gray stone on which her trembling head rested. The carved letters spelled a name. Falkener. Her name. I couldn't see the rest, my view obscured by her body. This was the grave of someone she'd loved.

If I'd been paying attention, I would have known they were coming. But my attention was all on her, the weeping Fehr commander in a heap on the mushy ground. The long, high-pitched, creak of the cemetery gate was my only warning. She spun toward the noise and saw me—

crouched and ready to spring upon her with my weapon drawn. Her guardsmen were filing into the cemetery and rushing toward us.

"It's you," was all she said.

I bowed my head to her.

"Are these soldiers friend or foe to you?"

She stared up at me, her lips shaking. "I don't know what they are. Or you. Or me."

I took her tiny, cold hand in mine. "Come with me. I'll get you out of here."

We ran through the muddy graveyard as the moon lay down behind the horizon. The black was upon us. We were blind. Good.

I moved through the night by instinct, guiding her beside me. I had no plan. I just knew I had to get her alone.

CHAPTER 10

LEUKA FALKENER

He pulled me along at a sprinter's pace through the black. My savior. He had appeared in the darkness like a newborn star, sparking into existence to light my path to safety. I had, after all, saved him as well. And though that day in the desert seemed like another life, I had felt him near me since. Flashes of him. His furious eyes boring into my pale skin like a sunburn, even when I was in my bedroom alone.

The skin of his palm was rough and hot against mine. I considered pulling my hand away. A logical thought. I almost listened to it. But logic had gotten me here, running for my life from the government I had served faithfully. And my father before me. I had ignored every instinct I'd ever had, trusting only proof. But proof had come too late this time. I'd killed for them, would have died for them, for the "greater good" they had convinced the universe they served. It didn't exist. Corruption and oppression—that was their way. Not mine.

So I ran with him through the falling rain, so fast that the drops seemed to hang motionless in the air as we burst through them. It was hard for me to keep up with him and every few minutes I felt a hard tug on my hand as he started to pull away. It wasn't the speed. He was fast, but on a sunlit morning I could run circles around him. It was the blinding darkness that made me doubt my every footfall, as if the ground may have disappeared from beneath me. He moved through it like he could see in the dark, his instinct like magic to me. When the city lights peeked through the night I pushed my legs harder and ran beside him instead of letting him pull me along behind.

I didn't know where he was taking me. Didn't care. He could be leading me right to the Ministry Council chambers to be tried and executed for my treachery. He didn't. Instead we ran, soaked and shivering, into the southeast corner of Dega—the capital city of the Ministry Empire. I'd seen the west side—where the council chambers and military memorials gleamed like ornaments along the street. That was the image they wanted to show, especially to other colonies. Comply with Ministry occupation and this could be your city. I'd seen the city center, where the factories stood tall and gray, like rows of haggard soldiers standing some immortal watch. The southeast wasn't something the council would advertise. Brothels, drug dens, violence. But it was probably the safest place in Dega for me. Ministry personnel and their guards weren't likely to sully their reputations by being seen in this place.

Then he stopped, so suddenly I nearly tripped over his big feet.

"Here, come on." He opened a swinging glass door

and waved me into the little building. The front was glass, allowing a view inside from the street. It must have been commercial once. Inside it looked dark, but it was hard to see through the dirty glass, grimy handprints covering them like a cave painting.

I stepped inside, scouring the dark room for any presence, but there was no one there but us. A thick layer of dust covered the counters and tabletops. Mechanical drones hovered overhead like a floating chandelier. They looked old and frightening in the dark, like flying robotic beasts summoned from a time long past.

"What is this place?"

"Drone Diner. The Silvernails came up with the idea a few years back. No human employees to pay, all profit. You just push the buttons on the drone to order and they serve your food."

"The richest family in three systems and they can't afford to pay waiters? And Reed, from the Triad, she's the youngest daughter, sent me to the desert with table scraps for the indigent. You'd think they might put more focus on job creation."

He stared at me for a moment. I didn't get it at first.

"Would you think that? Still?"

I shook my head, the cool skin of my cheeks warming as I realized what a naive thing I had said.

"They wanted your people starving. They wanted to force you into the factories to work for them—for us. For the Fehr."

I slid into a corner booth and one of the large mechanical drones floated down into my eye line. It looked like a stingray, even moved as if it were swimming, only more jerky and robotic.

"These things were a flop. Clunky and slow, too many

bugs to get too popular, but no one bothered to tear them down. They still make a few bucks here and there, and it's not costing them anything to maintain. They'll leave it here 'til it rots."

"But drones are illegal. They cause too much pollution and waste."

"They're illegal on Fehr. The Ministry doesn't care if they pollute their colony planets."

"I let them blind me," I muttered to myself.

He stretched his big hand across the table and lay it over the top of mine. I felt I was going every which way, all of the bits of me fluttering off in a sandstorm, disappearing on the wind. But his hand was solid enough to hold me down, to keep me in one piece.

"Get something to eat and drink. I'm going to find us some clothes and supplies. If anyone comes, get out of sight and be quiet. The only people who come here don't wanna be seen. Slavers selling girls and dealers selling synthetics. Sometimes junkies who need a place to crash."

I didn't want him to go. But I didn't want him to know I didn't want it. So I let my face remain blank and nodded.

Get myself something to eat? I thrust my hands into the pockets of the black coveralls I'd stolen from the guard. They were empty.

When I looked up, he was dropping a handful of Ministry credit coins on the table in front of me, as if he'd read my mind. Then he jogged out of the diner, his step light. He wasn't afraid. Not of the Ministry or the fugitive girl he'd decided to befriend or the execution he would face if he were caught. He was brave. Or stupid. Maybe both.

I didn't feel much like eating. But he was right. I would

need the energy. I ordered a sandwich, juice, and a red banana—I loved the things and this was the only planet where you could find them—and stuffed the coins into the little slot on the drone's back.

The door swung open, its old metal hinges singing along with the sigh of the cool outside air swooshing into the stale dining room. My body reacted. I didn't even look toward the door. No time. I catapulted up out of the booth and flipped over backward to land on the back of the largest of the drones. He hung high above the little booths and close to the cheap yellowing ceiling panels. I floated my hand over his control panel and with my telekinesis tore apart his metal guts. The last thing I needed was this guy floating down to serve a table with me curled up on his back.

I breathed slow and shallow, relaxing my muscles into stillness with every exhale. The voices that came from below were hushed, urgent. I didn't dare look down at them, afraid to peek my face over the side of the drone's massive wing and reveal myself.

"Are we alone?" I knew that voice. When he spoke, I pictured fluorescent lights and a gleaming shark-tooth smile. Benedict Vaughn, councilman of the Minister's Triad.

"It's empty." The second was a woman. Familiar, that voice. Stern and haughty, but I couldn't place it. I heard them move, sit down.

"Must we meet in this scum den? I'm not one of the desert whores you sell in the back alleys."

"I don't sell them. I have men to do that. And I wouldn't be seen in a place like this if you hadn't requested absolute secrecy." He sounded offended.

Selling women. Teeth would do anything to get closer to

money and power. Nothing would surprise me from that moment on.

"How could you let this happen," the woman said.

"Me? You chose her, said she could be used like a pawn. What of that?"

She almost hissed her anger.

"Anyway," he said. "We can contain this. It's only one factory."

"Contain it?" I heard a dull thud, like a fist slamming down or a foot kicking a wall. "The word has spread. The laborers in three other factories have already revolted."

"So we seek them out and punish them…destroy them. Make an example," Teeth said.

"If we destroy them, we destroy our entire labor force. No. It has to be the girl. The Red Lily. She is their hope. So we crush her."

The Red Lily. The symbol on the medal they had pinned on my chest—I was the girl they spoke of. The one they would crush. Reed Silvernail. It had to be her. Two thirds of the Triad sat below, plotting my execution. My shoulders ached from crouching like a crow on the drone's back.

"Say the word and I'll make her the most infamous fugitive in the universe. Her face will light the sky of every planet with a Ministry presence."

"Do it. I want armed guards searching every building in the city, residential or otherwise. Kill anyone who objects. Kill anyone who helps her. Hell, kill anyone who speaks of her favorably. There's your *example.*"

I heard the whine of machinery as the drone that had taken my order floated out of the back room. Beneath me it flew toward the table where I had been sitting, my food freshly prepared and resting on its back.

"We're not alone," the woman shouted. I heard the familiar sound of blades against fabric as their weapons slid out of wherever they were sheathed. Then footsteps, quick and rhythmic against the stone floor. Sweat rolled down my forehead, stinging my eyes through the slit between my squeezed-shut eyelids.

"Who's there? Come out and you'll die quickly. Take your time and I'll take my mine when I find you," she called out to every dusty corner.

The footsteps moved in every direction, down each row of booths, to every table. It wouldn't be long. I slid my hands to the front of the drone, muscles coiled like a snake and ready. When their steps were beneath me I would jump. Hopefully I could catch them by surprise, take one out with my landing and somehow fight off the other. If I didn't break a bone during the fall.

They were getting closer. I listened, every nerve in my body reacting to the sounds and nothing else. My other senses disappeared. I slipped a hand down to the belt of knives strapped around my thigh, the edge of my thumb skimming the cool bone edge and resting at its razor sharp point. I focused hard and the knife shifted just a fraction of a millimeter, barely poking into the tip of my thumb. I was ready.

THE END

WE FALL

The Red Lily
Part III

CHAPTER 1

LEUKA FALKENER

My muscles twitched and popped, strained from stillness. I was crouched low on the back of a winged drone hanging from a restaurant ceiling and trembling with unutilized adrenaline.

The footsteps below grew louder until they were right beneath me. Two members of the Minister's Triad circled the empty diner. Benedict Vaughn and Reed Silvernail. They were hunting me. Probably sniffing the air like predators. I was a rabbit among wolves. My heart pounded so hard I was sure they'd hear it.

The footsteps stopped. I let my knives float free of their sheaths, keeping them close to my skin, but unencumbered and ready to fly.

Then a gust of damp air struck my face. The door had swung open.

"Oh, good. My food's ready."

It was him. My stranger. I still didn't even know his

name.

I heard heavy stomping footsteps. He stumbled, then tracked over to my booth and sat down with a heavy thud.

"Hey, you folks know where the manager is? Damn food took so long I had to go out for a smoke."

"It's just some junkie. Let's get out of here." I could barely make out her whispers from my perch. Then quick footsteps and the swinging of the door.

I started to move but his voice halted me.

"Wait," he whispered. It was so quiet I wasn't sure if it was him or a voice inside my head.

Still silence. It seemed to stretch out over a year, but I'm sure it was just a few minutes. My body was cramping, curled up, hidden on the back of my drone. Finally, he spoke again.

"They're gone. Come on down."

I rolled off the drone's back and landed in a crouch a few feet in front of him.

"How did you know I was up there?"

"Just knew."

I stood up just in time to catch the canvas tote bag he tossed at me.

"Change your clothes in the back. You should find something that fits you in there. I think we better take this to go," he said, wrapping my food in a large blue dish rag.

I pulled a button-up work shirt and some dark jeans out of the bag. The jeans were a little tight, and the shirt a little big, but it would do.

The back room was half kitchen, half assembly line. I threw the clothes on quickly, then took a look around for anything useful. I'd never been a fugitive before, but I guessed that some extra food and supplies might come in handy. I grabbed two small boxes of contained flames and several pre-made peanut butter sandwiches.

The wine rack stood in front of me, still fully stocked, though the liquor shelf was sparse and the cooler cleaned out of anything cold. I passed it twice. Alcohol had never really tempted me. I only ever drank wine at the military ball once a year, and then just a glass. Stocked up on food and fire, I walked back toward the door, paused, and turned back around. Without stopping to think I stuffed two bottles of red wine into the large pocket of the bag, then hustled back to the dining room.

He smiled as I walked out of the kitchen.

"Sorry about the clothes. I found them in a donation bin around the corner."

"No, they're fine. They're great."

I walked toward him, stopped way too close to him, and placed my arms around him and squeezed like I'd seen the desert dwellers do. I was stiff, uncomfortable, but it made me feel better somehow.

"Thank you," I said into his ear before I let him go and stepped back. "They'll be coming for me and they won't stop. You can't imagine what I've done."

He held up a hand, stopping my rapid speech.

"I saw you at the factory. That's why I followed you. You need help."

I shook my head, meeting his eyes and trying to keep my expression stern.

"No, thank you. I respectfully decline." I turned away from him but he caught me by my arm.

"Where are you gonna go that they won't be looking?"

Damn, he was stubborn.

"I don't know yet. Away. The desert." I looked at my soaking wet feet. I guess I had no plan, but I didn't really care.

"I know a place."

"No. You must have people at home who need you. Your daughter?"

He looked away when I said the word, like he didn't want me to see his eyes.

"She's not...she's just a desert girl."

"Oh. The way you fought for her, it seemed like she was someone special to you."

He was still for a long moment, staring off as if he couldn't hear me. Then he walked out the door and I stood there staring like an idiot. Had I said something wrong? I didn't move for a minute. Then he poked his head back in.

"Come on. I've got your food and I'm not giving it back unless you come with me." He waved the napkin-wrapped sandwich at me, a playful smile on his lips that didn't quite touch his dark eyes.

I smiled back. It felt foreign to my facial muscles, smiling. I hadn't smiled in days, weeks maybe. It was nice. I snatched the sandwich out of his hand and pushed past him out the door.

CHAPTER 2

LIBERTY RHODE

I crouched, my back pressed against the cool, splintered wood of the barn's outside wall. The sky was black, the moon hiding her glow beyond the horizon of this desolate rock. The slaver stomped around, kicking the sand with each step. I heard his every move, could see him in my mind, peeking around corners. His hunched posture. The sweat on his brow. He was hunting.

Women, girls, it didn't matter. They had been disappearing in the black. It started just after my father and brother were taken from our ruined farm to work in the factories at the city center. Slavers had come for me twice in the dead days that followed their exodus. I had buried them both in the dried-out fields, once fertile and overflowing with the crops that had fed my family. I would bury this one, too. Bury him in the black so deep the sun would never again touch him. Not even his bones. But not yet. I had to know where he was taking them.

The desert was sparse and without cover. It didn't matter yet. The lightless sky covered me like a black veil. I kept a good distance away so he couldn't hear my footsteps and moved slow, even though every piece of me was aching to sprint after him like a panther and pounce. It wasn't worth the risks. Revealing myself too soon. Losing the girls. So I crept after him as he moved deeper into the desert. He wouldn't go back empty handed.

I followed him for a couple more miles. He never knew he was being watched. It felt strange. I was a ghost, invisible as the wind. A shadow, dark as the night itself. I moved, light and quick and silent, like Raelon had shown me. Stalking him, my prey. We came upon a little shack standing alone in the desert, a small fire still burning outside.

He crashed through the door with no attempt at stealth. He was too bold. Stomping around and smashing doors like he was untouchable. Someone powerful was giving this man orders. He fancied himself protected. But not from me.

I dropped down to my belly in the sand. I had to stay back or the firelight would reveal me. *Let it be empty. Please let it be empty.*

The screaming cut through the night's silence and my hopes fell. He emerged with a young woman, probably in her early twenties. She was thin, but we were all thin in the desert. He had her by a handful of thick dark hair. She struggled, narrow arms swinging at him, but he kept her low and distant.

I felt like I might be sick, watching her struggle against him, her back contorting as she tried to twist out of his grip. But that's what a child would feel. Children had mothers to hold them when they cried, little friends to play puppy dogs and fairy princesses with. I couldn't be that. Not anymore.

She had fight in her. She twisted her body over and bit his thumb as it slid over her face.

"Dammit," he cried out and threw her to the ground.

He climbed on top of her and grabbed another handful of her hair.

"You work for me now, bitch."

He tore the white cloth at the low neck of her dress, exposing her breasts.

"Oh yeah, they'll pay good money for you. When those hopped up, tweaker slum dogs get their hands on you, you'll miss me."

I crawled across the sand and sprang to my feet behind him, just out of his reach.

"Get off her."

He spun his head around, still crouched over the woman like a panting dog. Scum. Ministry serving, entitled scum. The knife flew out of my hand before he could speak. Perfectly accurate, it stuck in the side of his throat. His hand shot to his neck to grip the pretty little piece of metal, gleaming in the firelight. I'd forged it myself. To think that little piece of steel could have so much power.

"Not so fast. That knife just slit clean through your artery, and right now it's the only thing keeping your blood from shooting out all over the sand." I shook my head in mock sympathy. "You can go ahead and pull it out, but you'll bleed to death 'fore you get anywhere near the help you need to save your miserable life. Now I gotta closure gun in my pocket, could fix you up real good, quicker'n a sand flea bites. Supposing you do what I say.

Now you just hold that knife real still and stand up."

He did just what I said. He was my puppet now, I could pull any string I wanted and he would move just so. I flicked his red nose with my little finger as he panted, his pink cheeks puffing out with each breath.

The woman jumped to her feet, covering her bared breasts with her arms.

"Kill him," she cried. "Please."

"No. He's gonna take me for a walk. Show me where he was heading before I interrupted."

He laughed. "I'll take you. But you walk in that place, you'll never leave. They'll take you in and sell you over and over again, until you die there, just another used-up whore."

I ran at him, kicked him hard in the groin, and he doubled over with his hands on his crotch.

"Careful now, you don't want that knife to shift too much, darlin'. I'll tell you only once to keep your dirty mouth shut unless I tell you to speak. Talkin' out of turn is bad manners and you do it again, I'm gonna cut your damn tongue out and make you wear it around your neck."

He nodded, still clutching the knife in his fist.

"Good." I jumped on his back like a playful child getting a piggyback ride. "I'll keep this blade still for you, that way I know we won't have any misunderstandings."

I hung on his back for a minute, adjusting myself into a comfortable position and placing my hand over the blade in his neck.

"Go on. You're dripping something fierce and I wanna make it where we're going before you bleed out on me. Giddy up."

CHAPTER 3

RAELON TOREK

"Raelon," I whispered as we tiptoed down the soggy path through the swampland. "My name's Raelon."

We were ankle deep in water already and the sky was just beginning to lighten to a deep blue instead of inky black. I had to hurry. The path to this island would be completely under water once the sun was in the sky. Though Tokino's reservoir was manmade, it was large enough to be an ocean and behaved like one. The only body of water on the planet, it was massive and when the tide rose, it covered this path in its entirety. It was only above sea level during the black.

"I'm Leuka," she replied.

"I know. Come on, Leuka, we're almost there." I pulled her by the wrist, but she yanked back, holding one finger up as if saying 'just a minute.' Then she raised the wine bottle to her lips and took a long swig. Her face scrunched up like a kitten sneezing every time she took a drink from it.

"Do you think that's wise? You're being hunted. You ought to stay sharp."

"Don't tell me what I *ought* to do. I've been doing what I *ought* to do since I was sixteen and now I find out it's all stupid and wrong."

She took another swig, scrunching her face up again. I snatched the bottle out of her hand and took a drink. She was making it way too easy to kill her. Trusting a stranger, becoming over emotional, impulsive, drunk. So why was it so hard for me to even think about doing it? The kitten face wasn't helping to inspire a revenge killing—that was for sure. I liked her. I tried to push it out of my mind, but that wasn't the way of the Shadowmen. Passionate, impulsive—these traits were in my blood. I had been raised to embrace them.

We finally reached the island. It was still dark, but had stopped raining. The air was warm. We could sleep comfortably on the beach without shelter. I gathered some wood together in a pile, bending down to stack it in a pyramid shape. From over my shoulder something flew, landing in the wood pile. I heard a loud pop and it burst into a roaring fire. The heat hit my face at once, knocking me backwards. I landed on my ass in the sand, feeling my face with frantic fingers to make sure my eyebrows hadn't been burned off.

Leuka burst into a fit of childlike laughter. "Contained flame. From the Dine Droner. The Drine Droner. The, uh, robot food place." She giggled some more.

"Be careful," I said as she stumbled close to the fire. I caught her by the wrist and pulled her out of danger. Her feet tangled together and she landed on her butt. She jerked her hand free of my grip before I could help her to her feet.

"I'm done being careful. I've been careful and calm and logical for my entire life. I've ignored my instincts and changed who I was. God, I would have cut off my head to fit in when I was growing up, you know?"

I said nothing, but I did know. I had broken myself down just to build a brutal, cunning, Shadowman warrior. At least she had believed it was for some kind of greater good. I knew what they were. Had always known. But I did what I had to do to survive. No. Not just survive. Part of me just wanted to belong. When Mom left, it was the worst. She was my only outside connection. The only one who accepted me as I was. But I understood. There was nothing for her after Dad died. She wanted to go home.

"Besides—I'm not as careless as you think I am," she said, interrupting my wandering mind. "I don't trust you, but I am safer here with you than out there with them. There's only one of you, and even drunk, I could take you."

"Is that so?" I hadn't seen this side of her. Her disguise, her armor, it was crumbling in front of me. All that modesty and coldness that her people treasure—it was disappearing. It was like she'd squeezed every drop of what made her who she was into an air-tight bottle and hidden it up on a high shelf. Tonight the bottle had broken open, and she was spilling out all at once.

I took another drink of wine, still staring at her crooked little smile. I couldn't look away. The wine bottle pulled itself out of my hand and floated upward until it hung just over her head and tilted, trickling wine into her soft parted lips. Then she snatched it out of the air with the speed of someone much soberer.

"Yes. That *is* so. I don't think you could kill me, even if you wanted to."

I began to wonder if she was right about that. Every time she stumbled I wanted to catch her, to keep her from falling. The way she spoke, even drunk as she was, I couldn't help but stare at her. She was smart—smarter than me. She was my equal and opposite, cool where I was hot, soft where I was rigid. Yet, somehow we were the same. With one exception. She was good. Entirely, unwaveringly, good. There was no one like her. I cringed, imagining what she would think if she knew the things I had done. The things I planned to do.

She placed her cool soft hand on my cheek. "Where has your mind gone off to? You look so far away."

"I've got a quilt in the bag. I'll make you a bed. No pillow, though, sorry."

She watched me with suspicious eyes, but didn't ask again.

I spread the blanket out over a dry area of sand, close to the fire. The stars had come around to light the sky. I couldn't see the sun yet, but it made its presence known with a yellow-gray glow above the horizon.

"Wanna go swimming?"

I turned around to find her skimming the water with her toes. I lunged at her, grabbed her around the waist and pulled her close, her back against my chest.

"Not in the swamplands. The open water of the reservoir is safe enough, but not here."

She looked up at me over her shoulder, her eyes wide and sweet and child-like.

"What's in the swamplands?"

"I don't know exactly. But the locals tell stories. Creatures older and more feared than the Shankers in the desert. They call it the cloud water. It's so murky you can't see them coming. No one ever goes in the cloud water. They say no man who has braved the waters has ever returned. Nor have their bodies."

She was gazing out over the water and clutching my arms tight around her waist. I shifted my foot back and kicked a stone into the water. She screamed and jumped back.

"You ass!" She shoved me with two hands, laughing. Our laughter filled the empty little island and it seemed no longer desolate and abandoned. It felt warm. Then we were silent.

She stared at me, her smile shifting into a thin line. She looked suddenly grim. I resisted the urge to pull her close to me, so close her head would rest against my chest.

"You should leave me here, tomorrow." She paused to look at the glowing horizon, the newborn sun brushing her face with the gentlest glow. "I mean today. They'll slaughter anyone who helps me. I heard them say it. You don't owe me anything, now. We're even."

I took another drink of wine, emptying the bottle.

"Even? Is that what you think this is about?"

"If not that, then what? What are you doing here, Raelon?"

I stared at her in painful silence, willing myself to come up with an answer. What was I doing? Was I waiting for the chance to cut her pretty head off? To bring it back to Moses? The thought of laying her head at his feet burned more than any brand. She was a force unto herself. The Fehr, the desert dwellers, they all loved her. It was why the Ministry wanted her, why her actions had inspired a planet to go to war. Not because she was the best killer, like Moses. She was meant to be followed.

"I'm here because of you. What you're doing, who you are. There's a reason those people bowed to you in the desert, in the factory. People aren't like you. They are awful. *We* are awful. Monsters. But they see you and they—we—want to be...good."

I dropped to my knee and bowed my head to her. The words came easily. I'd said them before—pledging my oath of loyalty to the Alpha. I hadn't meant it then. The words had been hollow, just a script I had to read to survive another day. But now they were truer than any words I'd spoken and I pushed them out with no thought or effort, as natural as breathing.

"One among the many, it is you that I follow. My sword is yours, be it sharp and gleaming or rusted and dull. My blood is yours, as it flows in my veins or is spilled on the ground. My heart is yours, be it beating or still. I pledge to you my breath, and am yours to command, until the day it flows no more, and every day that follows."

She sprang into my arms and kissed me. The force of her hit me harder than any punch I'd ever taken. I was a leaf blown by a hurricane, battered and spun against the beach and carried away on the crest of a wave. I was beyond repair.

Pulling her into my arms, my body moved without thought or direction. I had never belonged. Not anywhere. Not in my whole life. But I belonged here. I belonged with her. All my flaws, all my darkest deeds melted away in the perfection of that moment. I was not the sum of the things I'd done. I was myself. And she saw me. I was naked and exposed, my insides ripped out and on display for her, but it was worth it. I would have cut out my own heart, held it in my open palm for her to examine if that were her wish.

Instead I pushed her away.

"You shouldn't...I'm not..."

I shook my head, cursing my clumsy words when she collided into me, silencing me with her lips over mine. We toppled over into the sand, her delicate body above me, taking me captive. I held her tight, my hands gripping her lower back. This could not be real. She slipped her dress up over her head and threw it into the sand. I tried to stop myself, pull myself away, but she brought me back to her with that crooked little smile.

"Tell me to stop," I begged her, my warm hands sliding over the cool bare skin of her back. She was pale and pristine. Everything I'd ever thought of as perfect was now in my mind mundane and absolutely ordinary by comparison.

She shook her head back and forth.

"Please, Leuka. If you don't say it, I don't think I can..."

She put one finger on my parted lips.

She did not tell me to stop.

I wrapped my arms around her waist and lifted her up with me as I stood. Her legs squeezed tight around my waist and that messy tangle of strawberry hair fell over my shoulder and back as she breathed against my neck. I stroked her hair and her head fell against my chest as I carried her to the blanket I had laid out in the sand.

Seconds melted into minutes and hours and she didn't ever tell me to stop. Not once. Soon the sky was yellow and the water glistened in the morning light.

When she finally fell asleep, the sun was high and gold and lighting up her face like some precious metal. I held her for hours, afraid to move, afraid to breathe, to wake her. She might regret this in the morning and I would put off that moment forever if I could. As long as she slept in my arms, she was as much mine as I was hers. Every bit of bone, every drop of blood, every inch of callused and scarred skin was her kingdom.

CHAPTER 4

LIBERTY RHODE

I thanked him. Meant it, too. Never would have found it on my own. Leaned right in and whispered it in his ear before I grabbed the little handle of that knife in his neck and yanked it all the way across his throat. He tried to cry out, but all that came out was wet desperate gurgling as he fell to his knees. The blood came out in spurts. Arteries do that when you cut them. He tried to cover it with his hands but the blood seeped between his fingers, pouring down the front of his chest like a morbid red bib. I could time his death by watching those blood spurts. They grew rapid and weak as his heart faltered and finally stopped.

"Sorry. Won't be able to bury you after all."

I kicked his limp figure into the ditch. He splashed face down in the dirty puddle. It was so shallow that his butt and the back of his head were still sticking out, but I left him there just the same.

The building was a few yards away. I waited in the

shadows until another slaver returned, five girls following behind him with their hands bound together. Could have killed him right there, thrown a knife into his throat like the last one. I wondered if I was strong enough to stick one right down through the top of his head. Could I get through the skull in one strike to pierce his sick, traitor brain? Didn't matter. I wouldn't kill him. Not yet. Sure, I could save those five girls, but the ones inside would be left in the hornet's nest. No.

I tiptoed over as he opened the door and followed them inside, as if I were just another captive. There were five men. I couldn't fight them all. Not all at once anyway, and not face to face. Two of them herded us into a room with dozens of girls. They lay sprawled all over the floor like broken dolls, breathing heavy. Some of them flinched when the door opened, but most of them didn't respond at all. They stared off, numb to the world and everyone and everything in it.

"Take your pick, boys," one of the men said. "Let's initiate the new girls."

"Seriously? Boss doesn't care if we sample the goods?"

This one must be new. He'd probably be the easiest to take out.

"Boss don't care what we do to 'em, so long as they can work. And if you can walk, you can work. Just don't bruise their faces up. They're worth more pretty."

New guy walked up to me, bending down to get to eye level.

"Geeze, this one's just a little kid."

I bit my tongue inside my mouth until my eyes welled up with tears.

"I want my mommy," I whined, really laying it on thick.

"Show her how it's done, Beatty."

He shook his head and took a big step backward.

"That's sick, Ross. She's a kid."

"Not anymore. You take her or I will, and I'm not gonna be nice about it."

Beatty took my hand and pulled me forward a step. Warm arms wrapped me up from behind. Soft tan arms. A woman's arms.

"Please, she's a child. Take me instead," the stranger said, her voice cracking.

The one they called Ross stomped forward and struck her hard in the face with the back of his hand.

"You'll speak when I tell you, whore. Beatty take the kid. This one's mine."

He led me out of the room and down a dark hall. Pausing, he glanced back and forth and then jogged down a dark stairway, pulling me along after him. We came into a stone-floored basement. There was no exit, just a little window above us.

He closed the door behind him, easing it in slow, so it wouldn't make a sound. Then he pressed his fingers against the dirty glass pane and eased the window open. It was small, probably a tight squeeze for an adult, but I could have slid through with no problem.

"Get out of here, kid. Go find your mom."

When he turned back from the window, he found my knife at his throat.

"I got me a dilemma. You see, you've shown me a kindness. But that don't mean you ain't a slaving whoremonger son of a bitch." I paused to fix my eyes on his. I'd been speaking fast and high, each sentence running into the next. Now I lowered my voice, took a breath, and spoke each word slow, so he'd be sure to understand. "You do the bidding of great and terrible men to earn yourself some kind of status. I kill men like you."

He trembled before me. Little bitty me. The image of it was probably funny. It calmed me, trying to picture it. Big slaver asshole quivering in fear of all four feet and ten inches of me.

"This is my first day, I swear. My father works for Stone Fist. It was this or the factories. I had no choice."

"We all have a choice. I can choose to cut your balls off and feed 'em to your friend, Ross. Or I can let you climb out this window and go far away from here."

"Please," he said, his bottom lip still shaking.

"Go. Go far. Leave this planet, if you gotta, but just remember that if I ever see you again, I will cut you up until I can't recognize the face of the slaver that I let live."

I pulled the knife back. He jumped up and wiggled through the window so fast the metal had barely left his throat.

Good. Now there were four.

I crept back up the dark stairway. My feet silent on the stone steps; I moved so light, so fast. My body was on autopilot and I trusted it, like Raelon had taught me. But there was something else to it that he either didn't recognize or didn't admit to. Something animalistic about moving without thought or question, based only on instinct. I felt cold in my fury.

I heard them inside the rooms. Dumb shits. They had separated themselves for privacy, leaving just two men guarding the other girls.

The closest grunting noises led to where a dim light peeked out from beneath a door. I threw it open hard. The time for stealth was over. Speed was the game now.

Finish it and get the girls out before anyone else shows up.

The door banged into the wall like a clap of thunder. The man snapped his ruddy, sweat-speckled face around, startled. Time seemed to slow. That second for him seemed to me a lifetime. The woman beneath him struggled to cover herself with one arm. He knelt behind her, holding her neck by a single hand, his arm outstretched and pushing her toward the floor. The shitty fluorescent light reflected a white gleam in his greasy hair, his glassy eyes. Even the beads of sweat rolling off his nose glistened in that harsh artificial light.

It wasn't Ross. I didn't know his name. Never would know it. I threw the knife as he howled in surprise. The blade flew straight into his open mouth, stopping that howl short and emerging out of the back of his skull, pinning his head to the wall like some sick decoration.

The woman screamed. She couldn't help it— it was frightening, watching him twitch and bleed and die. It didn't bother me—wouldn't have bothered the other slavers either. Her screams wouldn't matter. She was nothing, property. But his howl—that would bring them running. I slid around the door frame and crouched in the shadow.

Pounding feet. It reminded me of the plains cattle running in the fields. But that was back when the fields had grass in them, not just dry endless sand. Back when Dad would scoop me and Lincoln up and run us back to the house, back to safety and away from the stampeding animals. But these weren't hooves I heard approaching, and there were no big arms gonna wrap around me and keep me safe. Those days were dead. Dad was dead. Lincoln was probably dead. And me? I was someone else, now. Something else.

"What have you done, whore?"

They were inside. I inhaled deep, pulling three more throwing knives from the strap around my calf.

The closest one had burst through and now stood with his back to the door. I should have thanked him for making it so easy. Instead I stepped out from behind the door and stabbed him in the heart. He dropped to his knees in front of me, bleeding all over the worn wood floor before falling down dead in the pool he'd made. The others were inside as well. I threw at them both, got one in the belly and he went down. Ross jumped out of the way, landing up on the radiator. I pulled out my last handful of knives and unleashed them as he dove off the vent, grabbing at the light fixture in the middle of the ceiling. One knife caught him in a pant leg, pinning it into the wall. He hung awkwardly, holding the light fixture with his leg outstretched and kicking like a rooster caught up in some chicken wire. I threw another knife at his legs before he could get down. This one stuck him to the wall, slicing through the thick flesh of his calf. He moaned.

I walked closer. He was panting, still clutching the light, afraid to let go and let the knife slice the rest of the way through the meat of his leg. I could stand beneath him where he hung, right under his belly.

"If you get me down, I'll let you go unharmed," he stuttered in between his panting breaths.

I looked at him for a moment, stunned.

"You'll let me go?"

There were no words to express my wonder and fury at his statement, at least none that I could think of. So I said nothing and sliced him from his chest down across his belly. Blood rained over me like some unholy baptism.

I wiped it from my eyes.

The woman was staring at me. She was motionless for several seconds, not even breathing. Then she seemed to wake up all at once when one of the bodies jerked. I'd only hit him in the belly and he wasn't quite dead. I approached him calmly, removed the knife from his stomach and replaced it in his chest. I did it slow, watching his eyes go from wide and strained to empty. She shook herself and pulled her clothes on as fast as she could move. The buttons on her shirt were uneven. I think she noticed but she didn't fix them.

She grabbed my hand and spit on the body of her attacker as we ran over top of him and back to the other girls. They were huddled together in the dark, holding one another. Some were crying. They were all afraid.

"I have a place you can hide. In the desert. Come with me and we can fight them together."

Some of them stood up. Some just sat there, shaking on the ground.

"You wanna stay here? Be my guest. Wait for more of them to come back. Let 'em turn you into whores and sell you for a profit. Or you could come with me. Fight back. I can teach you how. Someone taught me."

It seemed to take forever. Hours upon hours though it was only a few minutes. They'd been beaten down for so long, I thought maybe they'd forgotten how to move on their own. But eventually they stood. Every one of them stood. They didn't speak. I didn't speak. But when I walked out of the building, they followed me. Kept following. Until the sun rose overhead and we were safe in the empty desert.

CHAPTER 5

LABORER A-4992

Something had changed. We didn't know just what it was, but there was a feeling in the air. Like electricity. The enforcers were jumpy, reacting with violence to even the slightest offense. And there were more guards than ever, double what we used to have, walking us in and out at shift change.

L didn't sleep much at night. Mostly he just sat awake, scribbling. Page after page, front and back. He said they were letters to his family in the desert. I didn't have the heart to tell him they'd never reach them. That the same brown envelope had lain in the bottom of the mail bin every day since I'd arrived here two years ago. Writing them kept him going. So I just sat up beside him, kept him company until our bodies gave out and we slept the few hours we had left away from the factories.

It amazed me, a boy of ten knowing all those letters, all those words. Said his daddy had taught him. My pop taught me to push a plow, to dig a ditch, to shuck corn. But I did all that real well. Better than all the boys my age. I was big and strong and useful. And that was enough.

Even so, when I looked at those smudgy ink marks on that paper, I felt something stir inside. Longing. Like there was this whole world made out of those marks in ink on paper that I would never be a part of. Mysterious and powerful as a magic spell.

I stared at them, night after night. Watched him dip a sharpened stick into a tub of black over and over again, until he finally piped up.

"I could show you how…if you wanted," he whispered.

I could barely hear his little voice over the snores of the other men in our room. Nine total. Was ten last week. 'Til the guards took J away from the factory floor. He didn't come back. They never came back. So it was nine.

I smiled at L and nodded, my shadow moving up and down the stone wall in the firelight. We had to be careful not to speak loud or too often. There were ten hours out of thirty that we weren't in the factories. The others liked their sleep and wouldn't be too friendly about having it interrupted.

So we whispered. Night after night, he showed me how to make the letters and the sounds they made and how to put them together to make words. Soon I could write well enough to scribble notes to him, slide 'em his way on the workbench when the enforcers couldn't see. My letters were sloppy and crooked compared to his. But sometimes the notes made him smile.

Tonight we sat reclined against the stone wall, using up the stubby end of my last candle to light our lesson. He was showing me where the dots go and when to use the big letters instead of the little ones.

"Seems like we should just use the little ones all the time. We use them so much more anyway," I said, sighing.

L giggled.

Then a man a few feet from us shot upright from where he lay on the floor. The sheet that covered him flung off as he flailed his arms.

"Kid, you better shut your damn mouth and go to sleep or I'm gonna shut it for you," he growled. His voice reminded me of the plow, its rusty blade dragging through the rocky soil.

"Sorry, mister," L whispered. "I don't sleep so good here."

"Then get some chemical assistance like the rest of us."

L shrugged. He didn't understand.

The man pulled a syringe of red fluid out of one of the shoes that stood empty by his feet.

"Synthetics. Red for sleep. Green to go all day and not dose off," he said, spinning the syringe in front of us. "I got both. Give you a good price just so the rest of us can get some shut-eye."

L reached his tiny hand forward. "It will really help me sleep?"

The man was leaning forward, syringe in hand as he stretched his arm out to pass it to L. I swatted it out of his grip in one smooth motion. L watched it fly, his eyes wide as it shattered against the wall. Glass shards and wet red drops formed a puddle by the wall.

"What the hell do you think you're doing, boy?" He was staring at me, red faced and cheeks puffing up like he was breathing heavy.

"He's clean. And he's gonna stay that way," I said.

Footsteps pounded outside in our hall. Guards were making their rounds. Our noise must have drawn their attention. The door whined as it swung open.

"Who wants to tell me why I'm hearing talking instead of snoring from this bunkroom?" he said, leaning in the doorway.

No one spoke. I shoved my back off the wall where I'd been reclined and lay down on the floor, pulling my sheet up over my body. L watched me for a moment before doing the same.

"I have to open this door again and they'll be floggings all around," he said, and then slammed the door back shut. I pinched the flickering candle out between my thumb and forefinger before rolling on to my side and squeezing my eyes shut. I waited there in silence, expecting payback in the form of violence. I'd destroyed that man's drugs. They didn't take that lightly around here. But the guard had been firm. Maybe he wouldn't risk it.

I didn't sleep that night. Just lay with my eyes closed and my fists balled, waiting.

CHAPTER 6

LEUKA FALKENER

The sun shined warm on my skin and I wasn't sleeping anymore. And I wasn't twenty-six anymore, either. I was eight years old and I was wide awake and running barefoot along the banks of the White River on the only planet I had ever considered home. Fehr. I lunged forward, grasping with both hands for my slippery prey. He wriggled in my hands, desperately trying to hop away, but I held him tight and stroked his red head with my index finger.

Red frogs were the trickiest. And the only ones I bothered catching anymore. The green ones were slow, the blues dull-witted. They were too easy. Reds were smart and dangerous. My hands were already covered in red splotches from their toxic skin. It was itchy and a little sore, but I didn't care.

I walked along the river, admiring my catch and wishing the seconds would tick by slower. I'd have to let him go soon. Free him back into the wild waters to live out his destiny as he should. I held him up to meet my eyes.

"It was lovely making your acquaintance. I can only hope that we will meet again someday," I whispered.

"Leuka? What are you doing?"

I turned to find the source of the interruption, my grip loosening enough that my red frog friend leapt from my hands to the freedom of the river below. The voice had come from Philip, a skinny runt of a boy who sat behind me in class.

"I'm catching frogs. Or I was until you messed me up."

"Oh. You're not supposed to do that. My mom says it's 'unseemly,'" he said.

"What's unseemly?"

"Don't you know anything? It means it doesn't *seem* like it's something you should do."

I rolled my eyes. "But who cares what it seems like? What are you doing out here, anyway?"

Philip started pacing around me in circles, his hands busy fiddling with something in his pockets.

"I wanted to talk to you. I wanted to tell you that I will let you be my girlfriend if you want to."

I started to pace as well. We walked in weird little fidgety circles, neither of us looking at the other.

"Well, what will I have to do?"

"If you're my girlfriend we get to sit together at lunch and recess. And I have to carry heavy stuff for you, because I'm the boyfriend," he answered.

I giggled. "But I'm *way* stronger than you."

"Are not."

"Am so. Should I carry heavy stuff for you?" I asked.

"No, that's not how it works. Never mind that part."

He stopped pacing, looked up at me with a sheepish half smile, and took my hand.

"Ow, Philip! I've got frog rash!"

I jerked my hand away.

"But we're supposed to hold hands. Anyway, if you're going to be my girlfriend, you've gotta stop catching frogs and getting in fights with boys. I don't want a girlfriend that's all unseemly."

I took a step backward. I'd have to think this over. Catching frogs and fighting with boys were my favorite hobbies. I wasn't sure I wanted to give them up just to be scrawny Philip's girlfriend and carry his school books around.

Philip darted forward like a predatory lizard and pressed his lips against mine. His were cold and dry. He didn't seem to enjoy it very much. It was more like it was a chore that had to be done. I thought he was probably only doing it because it was *seemly* or something.

His lips had only left mine for a second when I cocked back my fist and threw it hard into his nose. It was simply a reflex. Everything inside me seethed with anger, that this whiny brat was telling me what to do and touching me without my permission. He flopped backwards in the soggy meadow grass, his feet flying up over his head, a drizzle of blood running down out of his left nostril.

"I don't want to be your stupid girlfriend," I cried, sprinting away from him toward my home. Tears were welling in my eyes and I wasn't sure if it was because I knew the trouble I was about to get into or if it was something else. Something deeper. Maybe the realization that Phillip's vision of a relationship wasn't just a silly child's idea. It was the tradition of my world. Loveless.

Logical. Utterly devoid of passion. In that moment I felt more alone than I ever had in all eight of the years I'd existed. Well...at least the ones I could remember.

Until I opened my eyes. And the sun was hot and sharp yellow, not dull and soft and white, the way it looked from Fehr. I could feel it. Like a physical presence touching every exposed inch of my skin with hot, rough hands.

Hotter still was the hand—the real hand, the man's hand—that came down on my bare back. I jumped at the touch, unable to understand why the sun was so high when I'd only just woken up and why anyone with such big warm hands would have occasion to touch my bare skin.

I looked at him.

His hand shot off my back and floated up in the air next to his head. Defensive. Then I noticed my knives. Six from each of the leather holsters still strapped around my bare thighs. They floated at my sides, razor sharp tips gleaming in the harsh midday sun and pointing straight at him.

His eyes were wide, but remained on mine. Not on the knives hanging in midair. Not on my body, pink and sticky from the hot sun. I brushed away the sand that clung to me with short, frantic strokes.

"Why am I outside? And naked? Why am I naked?"

He shook his head, the corners of his mouth twitching as if he was trying to hide a smile.

"You're not naked, Leuka. You've still got thigh holsters on. You insisted on keeping 'em. Being that you're a fugitive and all."

The sleep began to float away when I looked at his face, the smile he tried to hide in those dark furious eyes.

I couldn't help but smile back. Then his words made their way from my ears to my brain.

"Fugitive? Oh, right. The factories." I dropped my head into my hands and as I did, my knives floated downward like leaves in a breeze and settled back into their homes. "I started a war. Raelon, what the hell am I going to do?"

He reached toward me, moving slow, the way people do when they try to pet wild animals. Careful. Don't startle it. Might run or kick or bite.

His hands touched my shoulders, so soft at first I barely felt them. He left them there a second. When I didn't run or kick or flay him with telekinesis, he pulled me in to his chest and wrapped his arms around me.

"You're going to fight. And if I'm right about you, you're going to win."

I pulled back, placing my palms against his chest to hold the space between our bodies. I felt my eyes widen as I stared into his.

"Last night…did we…?" *Fornicate,* I wanted to say but couldn't force the word out of my mouth. Not while my cheeks were burning red and his eyes were locked on mine.

"We did. You don't…?"

Remember. I could hear the word as if he'd said it aloud. His head dropped, eyes fell to the sand.

"I do. I just…was I…?"

I snapped my mouth shut before I could finish. I was a military commander, not some teenager in need of validation. But he answered anyway, nodding his head up and down for emphasis.

"You were…" His mouth hung open, head still nodding up and down while he searched for the word.

He never found it. Instead he just let out a long sigh.

I smiled. For a second. Then my brain kicked in. I snatched my pants up off the sand and shoved my feet in.

"Well, it was probably a mistake. The alcohol. You know." I shrugged.

He touched the tip of my chin with his fingers, bringing my head up to face him.

"It wasn't."

His eyes looked black against that burning yellow sun. There was no smile in them now. Just emotion so raw I almost had to look away. I wasn't used to this. To people expressing pain and joy and affection without shame. Without fear or judgment.

"It wasn't?" It's all I could say, a smile forming on my lips as the words came out.

"Not for me, it wasn't. And I know mistakes. I'm starting to think most of my life has been one big series of them. But not last night. I fell in love with you last night."

He leaned in to kiss me, his eyes half closed. I pushed him away.

"Fell in love?"

"Yes." He said it with no shame. No blush in his cheeks, no averting his eyes.

"In one night?" I was squinting. Like if I looked hard enough some evidence would appear, and this would all make sense.

"Yes."

His eyes were big and softer now. I couldn't look at them. Just shook my head back and forth, back and forth. "I can't…I can't…"

"I know." He took my head in his hands and it stopped

shaking. "It's okay. I don't expect you to feel the same."

"It's not that. It's just—that word hardly even exists where I'm from. I didn't hear it spoken until I was fourteen. It was treated like a bad word."

"You came from a cold world. I came from—"

"Here," I said.

He looked away.

"You are so damn beautiful," he said.

"Beauty fades."

"Not the kind you've got. I'm gonna take a walk. Give you some space."

He stood up from the sand. The second his hands left my skin, I missed their presence. I wanted to tell him not to go. That I didn't want space. Not if it was in between him and me. I didn't want anything between him and me. But these were emotional thoughts. Illogical thoughts. The kind I'd always been taught I shouldn't have. So I kept quiet and tucked them into a corner of my consciousness, as I'd grown so accustomed to doing, and watched him walk away from me.

CHAPTER 7

LIBERTY RHODE

This one would hurt. Worse than the first. Worse than the dozens in between.

"This water isn't safe," Tana whispered.

I glanced at her for a split second before wading in. The swampy muck seeped into the fabric of my pants, weighing them down so they sagged around my waist even more than usual.

"There are beasts in the cloud water," she called from the soggy ground at the water's edge.

"Then shut your face so you don't draw 'em out," I whispered.

She took two slow steps forward, her bare ankles covered in the slimy water.

"We'll die in here. And no one will find our bodies."

I trudged back toward her, soaked waist high and thankful for it as the desert sun beat down hot and merciless.

"You'll wait here for me. Watch for Ministry scouts. They been out all over the desert this past week looking for the Lily. We need to find her first, you understand?"

"How do you know they haven't found her already? It's been over a week since the factories. She could have starved out here. Could have been captured already."

I took a deep breath through my mouth to avoid the scent of the foul green water that had soaked into my sagging pants.

"They want us scared. If they'd found her, it would be all over the skyboards. I bet they'd broadcast her execution to the whole planet. But there's been nothing. No word." I paused to gaze across the broad horizon, sand on every side with only the sun to set east apart from west. "She's out there. But she don't know this desert like us. She's on the run and scared, with the Ministry dogging her step. She'll help us, but we have to help her first."

She nodded.

"What if you don't make it through the cloud water?"

I was already walking away, already up to my neck, my feet sinking into the thick sediment below with every step. There was a time when it would have frightened me. The threat of death. The fabled beasts of the cloud water. But you can do almost anything when there's no other choice. Impossible things. Horrifying things. They just weave themselves into the fabric of everyday life.

"Monsters don't scare me none. Ain't a damn thing under this water that's scarier than me."

She stepped back onto the soggy ground and nodded. I lifted my feet from the mud and sank below the surface, eyes closed. It was like swimming through honey, the water was so thick. But honey was sweet. And this was foul and foggy and dark. More like bile. Or the green shit you cough up when you have a bad cold.

It seeped into my nostrils. I pushed my limbs through it, struggling with every stroke. Instinct was to panic. To struggle for the surface and emerge gasping. I did not. I moved as fast as the cloud water would let me, careful not to splash. He couldn't see me coming.

Raelon was a fool if he thought I wouldn't find him. I'd shown him this place. And I'd searched damn near every other place in the desert to find her. Because where I found her, he would be lurking in the shadows, ready to strike her down. If he hadn't already.

More likely he thought I was sentimental. Wouldn't come after him because he meant something to me. He did. He'd taught me a lot in the months we were together. But you could do almost anything when there's no other choice. Still. This one would hurt.

I brought my head above the surface, just enough to get my nose out of the water and inhale a big deep breath. I was still on course. Heading straight for the island. Then back below the surface to swim through the clouds.

Something long and smooth brushed along my ankle. Even then I didn't fear. I felt some strange kinship with the predators of cloud water. Surviving. Doing anything to survive in the dark and the filth that was their world. We were the same.

I felt it slide around my thigh, coiling, tightening around me like a hangman's rope. So I slipped my knife down from the strap at my wrist and somersaulted in the thick slimy water. When I felt its grip on my thigh ease I struck, slicing blindly into its slippery flesh. It felt like the belly of a fish, but it could have been the creature's back or side or tail for all I knew. Didn't matter. I just pressed down hard and pulled my knife along as fast as the thick water would let me.

A flinch. I felt it shudder and hoped it would give up. That I had proven too dangerous to be worth the risk. Instead I felt its thick body wrap around my torso and squeeze. Now we were spiraling downward. My lungs were burning, the air forced out of them. I wanted to gasp.

I didn't know which way the surface was anymore. The spinning got faster, the water colder as we moved farther and farther from where the sunlight could break through. My eyes popped open, unbidden. It stung at first. So much that I couldn't see anything. Then my eyes adjusted to the murky dark and I saw the face of the creature, reeling back, preparing to strike.

A hooded serpent's head, with eyes so green they seemed to glow in the dark. Eyes full of desperation. One of us had to die. That's the only way this struggle would end.

My right arm was pinned to my body in the creature's coiling embrace, knife still clutched in my right hand and digging into the tender flesh of my outer thigh. I slid a knife into my left palm, waiting for the creature to make its move. The seconds seemed to stretch out, as if time worked differently under the clouds. Then it launched that hooded head towards my face, fangs bared, mouth wide and primed to snap down on my skull.

My left hand shot forward at the same time. A dart through the bilious water, straight into the serpent's mouth. I didn't stop until my knife penetrated the back of its throat and popped out the other side. I was shoulder deep inside its mouth, fangs the size of my face on either side of my arm. It shuddered. Then stopped and didn't move again.

I thought of the slaver then, just for a second—the one I'd pinned to the wall in the brothel in much the same way that I'd killed this beast. We were born on this same rock to this same race of the same damn species. But I felt nothing killing him. I felt more for the beast.

No time to mourn or gawk at the creature, though its head was so large it could have fit my entire head in its mouth with ease. I yanked my knife free and swam for the surface. As soon as my head broke through, I sucked in a huge breath. My nostrils were still full of swamp slime. I blew them clean with a bull-like snort and tried to blink my eyes clear of the film that was blurring my vision.

"Hold on," a soft voice said.

Two small arms wrapped around me and then I was being pulled along through the cloud water.

"What the fuck? Let go of me, I'm not drowning."

I struggled, kicking and flailing my limbs until I felt a pressure surrounding me from all sides. Like I'd been wrapped in a blanket so tight that I couldn't move a muscle except to breathe. Soon my feet dragged along in the mud and the sun warmed my skin. Someone picked me up. Someone else. Bigger arms this time. A dark masculine blur. Then I was lying on the beach in the warm sand. I could move again, and wiped at my eyes with frantic strokes until I could see.

And I saw him. Raelon. Stroking the orange-gold hair of the Red Lily. Holding her face in his callused hands. I tried to speak, but the slimy water had gotten in and I could only cough and sputter.

They both looked at me. I looked at Raelon, at the Lily, then back and forth again.

"Fresh water. From the stream at the other end of the island. There's bottles back at the camp." He spoke to her in a hushed, urgent voice. Then she was running. Her image just a blur of white and pink, a ghost vanishing into the distance.

Her footsteps faded. He was leaning toward their sound, listening hard. He didn't move until they were no longer audible.

"Libby," he said at last.

But I was already moving, somersaulting backward over my own head. Reaching my fingers up toward my forearm holster to pull a knife. But no blade met my fingers, only my own damp flesh.

Raelon held out both of my forearm sheaths, dangling them from his fingertips.

"You think I learned nothing from our first encounter?"

I pouted, just like I used to when he trained me.

His shoulders slumped just a bit. In that split second, I dashed forward and slammed the heel of my palm into his nose.

He lurched forward, grabbing his bloody face with one hand and swinging the other out in a wide arc to grab me. I ducked beneath it, rolled across his back and kicked him hard in the jaw. He was jolted sideways, but still didn't go down. This wouldn't be easy.

"Dammit kid, we need to talk, you and me."

He lunged at me, catching me in a bear hug that squeezed both my upper arms against my sides so tight it reminded me of the cloud serpent I'd just stabbed through the skull.

"Nothing. To. Talk. About." I pushed the words out in grunting, halted bursts, sucking a strained breath into my compressed lungs before each word.

I threw my head backward, knocking hard into his chin and then dropped to my knees in the same second. It worked. His grip eased just enough for me to slip under his arms and roll backward between his legs.

From there I kicked him just above the knee, causing his legs to buckle beneath him. He fell down onto all fours. I snatched my knives up from the sand where they had fallen.

"Nothing personal," I said, pulling out a knife with each hand. "But I can't let you kill her. She's the only hope we have."

I lunged forward, knife aimed for his heart, but he swatted me off course with one hand. Too direct. Easy to block. No room for error with him. I'd have to be perfect to win.

"Might interest you to know," he said, pausing to spin out of the way of my flying switch kick, "That I have no intention of killing her."

"You must think I'm stupid."

I waited. He was impatient. At least with me he was. He would make a move if I waited.

"I've never thought that."

Sure enough, he lunged, sweeping both arms together to catch me between them. I rolled beneath them, somersaulting to a crouch behind his back where I kicked my legs outward, sweeping both of his. He landed hard on his backside and I was already there, my knife at his throat.

"You can kill me if you want, but I'm telling you the truth. No harm will come to that woman. Not while I live and breathe."

"And why the hell should I believe that?"

"You've seen me lie, kid. C'mon. Am I lying?"

I shuddered. I didn't *think* he was. But everything depended on her. I couldn't risk her life. Not for anything.

"Why the sudden change of heart?" I pressed the knife down firm enough to make an impression while drawing no blood.

"I'm in love with her."

I laughed.

He was silent.

"Shit, you're serious?"

His head fell an inch. Face burned red. He was telling the truth.

I dropped my knife to my side and took a step back.

"So what, you brought her out here to kill her, but the moon and stars were so pretty that one thing led to another and you ended up knocking rocks all night instead?"

He got up from his knees and brushed away the sand that clung to them.

"Does it matter how it happened?"

"All of it matters. And she decided you were so charming she'd excuse you for stalking and planning to murder her?"

He didn't answer, instead staring at his fingers like they were the most interesting thing on Tokino.

"She doesn't know who you are, does she?"

He shook his head in silence.

I slapped him hard in the face, open handed, because it felt appropriate.

"You're a child."

"Says the eleven-year-old."

"I'm thirteen. Dick."

He grabbed my shoulders in his big hands, but I

shrugged them off. I didn't want his affection. He wasn't family. He wasn't anything to me.

"Libby, you can't tell her."

I stared at him for a long minute before my mouth could form words.

"And why the hell can't I? There is more at stake here, Raelon, than whatever the hell is going on between the two of you."

He put his finger to his lips.

I rolled my eyes.

"I'm going to tell her. I just need to find the right time."

"What happens when your Shadowmen buddies show up to finish your job for you? Or when you forget and take off your shirt for some reason and she recognizes your spirit brands? Find the time fast, Rae. She ain't dumb. She'll sniff you out for the rotten thing you are, just like a carrion crow."

"Shhhh." He raised his finger to his lips again. "She's coming back."

"I don't hear anything." As if queued by my words, soft footsteps sounded from far in the distance. "How did you know?"

"I could feel her."

"Bleh. Sick." I stuck my tongue out and made a gagging noise. "You sappy fuck. Now I want to kill you again."

CHAPTER 8

RAELON TOREK

"This isn't a good idea," I said. She ignored me, walking on ahead across the desert. Her shadow seemed to stretch out like an image in a warped mirror as the sun bowed down to kiss the desert horizon.

I jogged to catch up. "You don't know who these people are. They can't be trusted. Any one of them could give you up to the Ministry to save their skin."

"They need me," she said. She didn't face me when she spoke. Didn't even slow her pace.

"Damn right we do," said a familiar voice. Then she was there, the top of her head coming into view as she climbed over the nearest sand dune.

"Liberty. Thank you for agreeing to escort us," Leuka said.

"Wow. You talk even fancier'n your love muffin." She nodded toward me.

Leuka's head snapped around to face me, her forward march stopping so fast I almost ran into her back.

"What did you—"

"Nothing," I said, too fast. "I didn't tell her anything. She's…perceptive."

"You should let her finish the question. It's more convincing that way," Libby said, winking at me. Then she faced Leuka. "He really didn't tell me anything. I guessed."

She took off again in the direction she'd come from, motioning us to follow. Leuka jogged up beside her.

"And what did you guess, exactly?"

"That you two played a little horizontal hopscotch. Hey, I'm not judging. You've been out on that island a few weeks now. It gets cold during the black. Lonely. Personally, I think you could do better, but what's that old saying? Judge not…unless you be…a total dickbag or something like that."

Leuka laughed and shook her head. "Yeah, I think that's it," she said.

"Sometimes you seem so grown up, kid," I said. "And then you say something like 'horizontal hopscotch.'"

She glared at me over her shoulder, but couldn't hide the smile from her eyes. "Well what do you *grown folks* call it?"

"Making love," I said at the same second Leuka spoke.

"Sexual intercourse," she blurted.

We looked at each other for a moment. Her eyes were wide, cheeks red. Then she looked away and started walking faster. The silence seemed to stretch on for days until it was broken by a soft whimpering in the distance.

I ran ahead, looking for the source of the cries. It sounded female. Leuka caught me by the wrist and pulled me to a halt.

"Careful," she whispered.

Libby was walking toward us. She seemed undisturbed by the noises, her face casual. Once she caught up, she said, "We should probably keep out of sight."

She ran a few yards off to a smooth, wide sand dune that resembled a rolling ocean wave and dropped down to a prone position behind it. She lay still for a few seconds before waving us over.

We ran together, Leuka's fingers wrapped tight around my wrist until we dropped beside her, bellies down in the sand. From here we could see her. A woman. Tan and lean and curled up in a ball beside a makeshift tarp tent. She rocked back and forth, knees hugged in to her chest. She was crying, soft moans punctuated by the occasional loud sob.

"Shouldn't we—"

"Shhhh. Look." Libby pointed beyond the woman, beyond her little tarp tent, to where three dark-dressed figures approached from the north.

"Too dark to be Fehr. Are they Ministry Guard?" Leuka whispered.

"Nah. Slavers," Libby replied.

I popped my head up over the dune. They were far enough away. Plenty of time to get to her before they did. I pushed my hands down into the sand, getting to my feet.

Two hands, one small, one even smaller, came down on my back at the same time. Both women pushed me back down beneath the cover of the sand dune.

"We need a plan," Leuka said.

"No. We don't," Libby whispered.

"I had a plan. Kill the slavers. Save the woman."

"While I sit here and watch? That's not how it works. We need to work together."

"Did anyone hear me? We don't need a plan 'cus she don't need savin'."

Leuka dropped her forehead into the palm of her hand.

"Yes, I'm sure the sobbing, half-starved peasant can fight off three men on her own. We should probably just put our feet up and watch, right?"

Her voice was thick with sarcasm. But Libby just smiled and leaned back with her arms behind her head.

"Take a look," she said, pointing.

The slavers were close. They'd spread out, circling her. She was surrounded. She didn't even look up until they were within a few feet.

"Screw this. I'm going," I said, jumping to my feet.

"Just watch," Libby said.

When the woman finally looked up, she was smiling. Then out of the sand they sprang, three of them, like the desert itself was rising up to protect her daughter. The slavers didn't see them. And never would. Their throats were slit, blood pouring into the sand before they ever turned their heads.

"Where did they come from?" I asked.

"Underground. We have to keep out of sight. Ministry satellites can see everywhere. The camp is below."

Smart. I looked at Leuka, sure she would appreciate the clever approach. But she was still staring at the three woman warriors in the distance, now wiping blood from their hands and dragging the bodies to God knows where.

"Is that…?"

"Is it what, love?" I asked her, but she was already off. She jumped the dune and sprinted toward them, slipping in the sand once because her feet were moving faster than the rest of her.

"Cece," she called.

One of the women looked up, her tan face sharp and angular and full of shadow from the setting sun. But her eyes turned soft and sad when she saw Leuka flying toward her.

"My Lily," she called in return. She dropped the corpse from her arm and stepped on its chest as she broke into a run.

The women locked their arms around each other and held on. We walked down to meet them and, even when we reached them, they held their tight embrace.

"I was afraid the Ministry would arrest you. After what happened at the factories."

Cece looked down at her feet.

"Stone Fist held me for a day," she said. "I didn't answer his questions so he left me in the desert, bleeding. Said the Shankers could have me."

Leuka brushed the woman's long dark hair off her face.

"Bleeding? What did he do to you?"

Leuka's eyes were examining the woman, taking inventory of any damage inflicted. It was then that I noticed the angry red scar, still scabby and peeling. It streaked up from her chest to peak above the neckline of her dress.

She pressed her palms against the left side of her chest and her dress flattened down beneath them in the place her breast should have been.

"I was awake when he..." Her voice broke off and she looked away. "Liberty found me. Saved me from dying there in the sand."

Leuka gripped her friend's shoulders in her tiny white hands.

"This is my fault. I should have made sure you were somewhere safe before—"

The woman cut her off. "There is nowhere safe. Not until we drive them from our home."

"I will make them pay for this," she said, squeezing her shoulders so hard the other woman winced. "For everything."

She nodded, her jaw hard set and sharp.

"Liberty is teaching us to fight. To be strong."

"You were always strong, Cece."

"Hate to break up the heartwarming reunion, but we should get below," Libby said.

Leuka nodded, but didn't move her gaze from Cece's haunted face. I took her hand in mine. Her feet stayed planted in the sand until I tugged her gently toward me. Libby was already heaving open a hinged hatch, masked well by the desert floor. We followed her inside, leaving the women to deal with the remains of their slaver victims.

CHAPTER 9

LEUKA FALKENER

I followed the girl down through the hole she had opened up in the sand. It was narrow, like climbing down the planet's throat. I slid down on my bottom, crawling like a crab down the steep incline until the hole opened up into a tunnel. I dropped through, landing in a crouch beside her. She was already cracking a flash orb and orienting it above her head.

Raelon dropped down beside me. The hole was a tighter squeeze for him. He popped out feet first and landed in the dirt, a pile of limbs. I extended my hand to help him stand. He took it, brushing off the dirt with his free one as he stood by my side.

"This way. They're expecting you," Liberty said.

We followed her along the tunnel, passing by dozens of little rooms dug out of the dirt and lining the corridor. Dirt walls, dirt floors, some had a fabric sheet hanging on roots in the doorway. Some only had straw on the floor in the shape of a tiny, makeshift bed.

"What's this?" I asked.

"Our bunkrooms. We have to share. But we try to dig a few more out whenever we get new recruits."

"New recruits?"

"We scout the desert for slavers nightly. When we find them, a party will follow them back to the city and bring the girls back here."

"And the slavers?"

She stopped in her tracks, staring straight ahead. Raelon turned to look at me.

"The slavers? We kill 'em. We kill 'em all."

"Just kill them? No trial, no justice? They are your people, too." Raelon was shaking his head at me in silent warning, but it was too late. The little girl turned on me, her face suddenly appearing older in the shadowy orb light.

"My people? They beat and rape my people. They drag women out of their homes and sell their bodies like livestock. I'd kill every last one of them if I could and…" She paused to step forward, her face inching closer to my own, though she was a half foot shorter, "…anybody who thought they had the stones to stop me."

I took a step back.

"I'm not reprimanding you, Liberty. But this is a war. And every soldier you lose fighting slavers is one less you have to fight the Ministry. And you will need every resource available to win against the Ministry."

She took another step forward, a little wrinkle forming between her eyebrows as she spoke. "And what about the soldiers we gain by emptying the city's whore houses and bringing those women here to fight?"

Raelon stepped forward this time. "Scared, abused,

slave girls are not soldiers, Lib. You know that."

"Neither are half-starved factory workers, or peasant farmers. Or orphans."

He put his hand on her shoulder but she shook it off.

"Leuka's just saying that you need to pick your battles. Focus on the real enemy," he said, stepping close to my side and taking my hand in his.

"I know what she's saying. But she's wrong." Her voice was strong and clear, eyes narrow and focused. "You both are."

Then she strode off again. We followed, a few paces behind. I felt it might be good to give the girl some distance. Soon we entered a cavernous chamber, filled with the souls that would make up my army. Men and women, all skin and bone and big wide eyes that glistened as they clung to the sight of me.

"What now?" I whispered to Raelon. But it was Liberty who answered.

"Now you talk to 'em."

She sat back against the dirt wall, pulling a long cigar from her pocket and biting the end as she flicked a match.

"What do you think you're doing?" Raelon snapped before the match went out.

"Smoking. I found it on a dead slaver. Well, truth be told he wasn't dead 'til I got done with him," she said, eyeing me with a sideways glance as she spoke.

He snatched the cigar out of her mouth with one hand and put it out on the dirt wall.

"Hey," she yelled.

"You're just a kid, Libby."

"No she's not," I said.

Raelon stared at me, but I kept my eyes on Liberty.

"She's right. She's not a kid. Nor an orphan. Nor a

peasant farmer. She's a soldier."

Raelon glared. He'd never looked at me like that before.

"That's not our choice to make, Leuka."

"I know. It isn't hers either. It isn't a choice at all. She's a soldier. Give her back the cigar."

He sighed, but handed the cigar to the girl. It looked comically large in her freckled little hands. She didn't light it, just slid it into the pocket of her vest and leaned back against the wall again.

"Guess I'll save it 'til there's something to celebrate. Or I'm about to kick off," she said with a face-splitting grin, her eyebrows wiggling.

It was a gesture, I thought. Not smoking it in front of him. But he didn't seem to notice.

Liberty slid a gleaming silver blade out of the worn leather belt she had strapped around her arm and began sliding the pointed edge under each of her fingernails, flicking the little specks of dirt off the edge each time.

"Nice blade. Looks fresh forged," Raelon said.

She kept her eyes on her fingers and said, "Yep."

"I don't suppose this rebel camp of yours has a workshop with a kiln and raw steel."

She didn't look up. Didn't respond. Raelon was looking at me. I shook my head in silent warning, but he couldn't help but keep talking.

"Lib, you can't be running off on your own back to that barn in the desert. You'll get yourself killed. Or worse, you'll lead the enemy back to your camp."

I smacked my hand against my forehead, sighed, and wondered if this beautiful, foolish man had ever had an argument with a teenage girl.

"Thanks for your advice, Pops. Next time this army

needs blades, I'll just go pick some from off the weapon tree. I think it's out back next to the fountain of youth and the goddamn rainbow trail to fairyland."

Raelon opened his mouth, but I held up a hand to silence him. He looked hurt, but his lips fell shut just the same. He opened it one more time but I shook my head and he turned away in silence.

"You're up," Liberty said, nodding her head toward the crowd of would-be soldiers. "They need to hear from the Red Lily."

I nodded and inhaled deep into my stomach before marching over to the center of the crowd.

"I'll be right here," Raelon whispered as I walked away. I looked back, meeting his eyes for the briefest of seconds before turning away.

"My name is Leuka. You may know me as the Red Lily."

They stared at me. Silent. A sea of dirty tan skin and prominent bones speckled with sparkling wide eyes.

"You have sacrificed much to get here. Risked your lives, your freedom, your safety. I would like to tell you that the worst is over. But that's not the truth."

I looked back toward Libby. She was no longer reclining against the wall, but leaning forward, her face solemn.

"You left slave labor and intolerable conditions, only to trade them for dirt floors in a hole underground. And for that I am sorry.

"Food will be scarce. Same goes for water and supplies. And many of us will die before this war ends. Even then, we may not be victorious."

They were still. Impossibly still, like time had frozen with my bleak words. They were more scared than ever. Good. They had to know what this was—to truly understand the sacrifice they were making.

"I don't tell you this to scare you. But fear is appropriate. I am scared. I, like all of you, may very well die before this is over. I know this. And I choose to fight. Because this is a cause that is worth my life. This is a cause worth dying for."

They were nodding their heads. Some whispering to each other.

"The Ministry—the Fehr, they believe that some lives are worth more than others. That they can dominate those inferior beings. Own them. Own *you*. They will use this planet and everyone on it until there's nothing left but bone and stone and sand. Unless we rise. Unless we fight."

They were on their feet now. Yelling their approval. I raised my hands again, calling for silence.

"Decide now. Each of you. On your own. Because this will get harder. Will you go hungry? Thirsty? Unwashed and injured? Will you give your last drop of blood to the sand for this? If not, return to the city. Surrender and beg for mercy or hide yourself away. But I intend to fight. And I will not stop until the last of my blood is soaked into your soil or the Ministry is driven from this land."

Now they stood and cheered. And I let them. My heart racing, pounding through my rib cage with the honesty of the words I had spoken.

I walked back to Raelon. Liberty stood when I approached, cigar hanging from the side of her mouth, still unlit.

"Some speech," she said.

"Do you think they're ready?" I asked her.

"No. Are you?"

I blinked twice and willed myself to speak, to answer her in the affirmative. When my voice failed I hoped I could nod, move even just my chin. The smallest signal that I was prepared to go to war with my blood, to rage against everything I'd ever known and held as truth. But my head would not move, nor my chin.

Libby punched me on the upper arm and walked away.

CHAPTER 10

RAELON TOREK

The moon fell out of the sky, leaving it black and empty. The tide was low. It was time.

"Don't go," I said. "I have a bad feeling."

"I'm going. I have a contact on the inside."

I inhaled deep through clenched teeth.

"Why now? They're running your drills every day. They're actually starting to look like soldiers. And we're getting food and water out of the city through the tunnels. This is working."

She leaned close, laying her forehead against mine the way she did sometimes, like maybe if she put her brain close enough to mine, she could make me see it her way.

"Won't last. We need intel. We need to know where they're weak and how to hit them so it hurts just a little too much. Time is their ally, not ours. The longer we give them, the tighter they'll turn the screws."

"Then let me come with you."

She pulled her face back, just an inch from mine.

"No. I need you here in case I don't come back. You're the only one with any real experience in battle."

My pulse pounded harder, so hard I was sure she could hear it. It pushed a warm rush of blood up into my face and neck.

"What makes you think I've seen battle?"

She smiled, her eyes squinting as she cocked her head to one side.

"Really?"

I shrugged, watching her face in silence.

"Okay, I'll play," she said. "The way you move. You never cross your feet when you walk, always keep them wide, stable. The way you sleep easy on any old dirt pile, but wake at every noise the night makes. The calluses on your weapon hand." She paused, took a deep breath, and looked away from my face. "The way you breathe when we have sex…" She trailed off, her voice fading to a whisper. Then her eyes met mine again. "When we make love. Like it's the only time in your life you've felt so raw and passionate and physical with someone you weren't about to kill or be killed by."

I shook my head, trying, and failing, to smile.

"Go on then," she said, lifting my chin with one hand and forcing me to face her. "Tell me I'm wrong."

I said nothing.

"This desert has a way of hardening people. You don't have to tell me what it was. But don't treat me like I'm fool enough not to see it."

I shook my head. She was no fool. The sand was warm and comforting against my bare feet. I crouched down into it, reclining back against a mound. Once there may have been trees or reeds or bushes growing up out of it. But now it just jutted out of the desert, full of dead roots.

She knelt to kiss me where I lay. Her lips were warm and soft. I kept my eyes closed, holding on to that kiss. When I finally looked up, she had reached the road. I watched her pale skin disappear into the void of black like a ghost.

I would wait, just long enough to let her cross the swamp road. Everything I had ever been taught was screaming at me to let her go. There was no happy ending here. I was not worthy of her. I was no good. She would run screaming in disgust and fear if she learned what I really was. When she learned. I could only cling to the shadow for so long. And I felt catastrophe looming over us, ready to drop at any moment, as real as the sand beneath my back. It would be kinder to leave now. I could disappear in the night—run from her and spare her the pain that would come with the truth.

Even as the thought entered my mind, I knew I would never leave. Because even if she hated me, I would serve her until my last breath. She was more than a lover. I believed in her, in her cause. This had become my war, too, and I meant to win.

I jumped to my feet and sprinted toward the swamp road to follow her. She was just out of sight. If I ran the whole way, I could make it before the path was washed over with thick swamp water. As soon as my feet hit the soggy path, the water crashed in from either side. Twin tidal waves forming out of the mist in the air as if enchanted. I dove back onto the island, wet from the knees down.

"Dammit, Leuka," I cried out loud. It was too soon for the tide. She had done this so I wouldn't follow.

I sat cross legged in the sand and stared off into the void where she had disappeared. I couldn't see anything, but I didn't blink. Watching. Listening. There was nothing there. But I felt something.

I kept staring forward, as still as the night itself. What I felt made my skin crawl like a thousand tiny insects scurrying over my body. A presence from my past. When I imagined his face, ever bathed in the Alpha's shadow, I could still taste scorpion venom, feel its sting on my tongue. For the first time, I was glad Leuka had gone.

"Bishop? I know you're here."

I heard the water stir as he no doubt slithered or crawled whatever vermin form he had taken out of the swamp and onto the sand. As he shifted, I could see nothing. My blindness made the noises that much louder, the shifting of bones and skin, snapping, popping into place. I jumped backward when I saw how close he was, the whites of his eyes floating in front of my face like two iridescent ghosts in the black.

"Where is she, Raelon? Where's the girl?"

I threw a quick punch to his jaw, but he collapsed into a waterfall of skittering beetles before my fist made contact. Then I heard his body reforming behind me, spun to meet it.

"What do you want with her?"

"Her head. What else? To place next to yours at the Alpha's feet."

"She's mine. Mine to kill. My mission. Be gone. Go back to the hole you slithered out of."

I shoved him hard and he stumbled backward.

"She's yours? Isn't that sweet. The Alpha knows of your treachery, Raelon. Bedding a pale. Plotting against your own kind. He's called for both your heads."

I struck at him fast, before the last word had fully left his lips. The thought of him touching her set my insides on fire. I struck fast and blind and my punch landed hard, sent him reeling before he could shift again. He stumbled back, falling. But before he hit the sand, he was shifting into a swarming cloud. I watched, listened, and kicked out at chest height as soon as I heard his bones popping into place.

He fell to the ground in transition. The shape of man, but made up of crawling bugs. I stomped on his ribcage and he let out a sound I'd never heard a man make. Something between a groan and a hiss. Kneeling over him, I took his neck in my hands and squeezed.

"Where are they?" I shouted.

He moved his lips, but no air could escape the tight grasp I held on his throat. His eyes rolled toward the east in the direction of the desert and Libby's barn.

"They traced my ship?"

He struggled to nod his head up and down. I squeezed tighter.

Don't let him go. If I eased my grip for a second, he would shift. I held on as he struggled for air, writhing and twitching against my iron grip. Leuka's face was in my head. I had brought all this on her. My kind. Scum like me hunting her in the night. I squeezed tighter. I had to kill it, this foul, evil thing had no place anywhere near her. This killer.

His skin was turning blue. I began to see my face instead of his, my hands around my own neck. She didn't know this side of me. Murderous, vengeful, violent. I tried to squeeze tighter. But she was with me. Her eyes, her hair, it was all I could see, staring at me in horror. Or worse, turning away from me in disgust. My hands slid off his throat and he disintegrated. A million tiny insects vanished into the sand.

Stupid, Raelon. I should have killed him. Now he'd wasted my time. The swamp road was washed over. I wouldn't be able to pick up her trail. She'd be safer in the city. Safe from my kind, anyway. They didn't know where she was and wouldn't go running into the Ministry Capitol, a city swarming with their enemies.

I had to get back to the desert. My ship would lead them right to Libby. She slept in the camp, with the rest of the rebellion. But it was close enough to the barn where my ship was hidden that she still visited when she could get away. She had a workshop in the back where she did her metal work. And last time I had seen her, she had a dozen fresh-forged throwing knives. If she was there when my people came…I couldn't think about that. I just had to get there first. I had to cut them off before they hurt Libby, before they found Leuka.

I stuck one foot in the cloud water. Cold. Thick. The smell of decay wafted up as I disturbed the water. Libby had nearly died from her swim across, and that had been in the light of day. I couldn't die. There would be no one to stop them. They would keep coming. Over and over until they found a way to get to Leuka.

I sat cross legged in the sand, eyes locked on the cloud water, waiting. Waiting was not something I did well. My thumbs drummed against my thighs as the seconds ticked by, each one grating at my nerves a little more than the last. The water just had to go down a bit. Enough that I could wade through. Leuka's man-made tide would recede when she was far enough from shore. She couldn't hold it all night. I just prayed it would go before the real tide came to meet it.

The sun had already started to peek out from the horizon when the water reached my waist. It was enough. It had to be. The tide rose with the sun. It was as shallow as it would be until the next black. I waded in and pushed my way through. Get to the ship. Get to Libby. Stop the Shadowmen and save Leuka.

CHAPTER 11

LEUKA FALKENER

I ran so fast it felt like flying, silent as the night wind. Slowing down was not an option. If I paused to take a breath, I might run back to our island. Back to Raelon's side and stay hidden from the world of my past, which had already crumbled to ruins around me. But I had to face it. I was at war with the Ministry. Favors would be called upon. Secrets collected like fossils, dusted off, and used when the time was right.

Still, I wished I'd told him. There was a feeling writhing around in my gut like something living and small and monstrous. I didn't know what it was exactly. Fear, maybe. But something more specific. I told myself it was all right. That I'd tell him later. That he'd made me feel like no one ever had. He made me feel trusted and wise and certain of my actions.

I wanted to say it before. That I loved him. But my

cold Fehr blood wouldn't let my heart speak. So I left him alone on our island, still wondering. I decided in that moment, feet pounding along the moonlit alleyways of Dega, I would tell him. I would defy my blood and my upbringing, ignore my fear, and say the thing that was ready to claw its way up from my gut, wrench my mouth open and leap out.

I was outside the Ministry Headquarters before the sun started to rise. The lower level councilmen and women were housed inside, given luxurious chambers with maids and assistants. It was considered a benefit, but Avia had shown me the truth of it. They kept the ones they didn't trust close.

I had been working all week on a way in. It was risky and would take all my focus and every bit of telekinetic energy I had. Even then I wasn't sure I could pull it off. Creeping to the back side of the round white building, I saw it. The skylight, glaring out at the rising sun like a single, all-seeing eye. It led straight to the vipers' den, the council chamber.

My body melted away from my mind, relaxing so fully that the molecules in my skin seemed to stir about with the particles of air around me. They spun and buzzed until I couldn't tell where I stopped and the outside world began. My mind watched it all, felt it all, from somewhere beyond. A puppet master readying to pull her strings.

I closed my eyes, imagined my body and pushed. Slow and shaky, I started to rise. I lifted myself to the height of the roof. Opening my eyes almost did me in. I trembled in the air, dropped like a floating leaf when the wind dies. But I caught the edge of the roof with the barest tips of my fingers. One by one, I shifted each of them forward, gaining more ground until I had a firm hold on the edge with both hands. Then I bent my elbows and lifted. I didn't know what was harder, lifting my body with my mind or my muscles. I felt like my arms were about to rip out of their sockets, but I kept pulling.

When my chin reached the edge, I threw one arm over, then the other. Next a leg, swinging my whole lower body from side to side until my foot hooked up onto the roof. I pulled myself up, lying still for a second, panting.

As my breath slowed, I crawled my way over the rough black shingles, gritty like sandpaper against my palms. Black as they were, tiny flecks of something shiny in them glowed, reflecting the pale light of the moon. Little bits of light in a world of dark. I made my way to the great round skylight in the middle of the roof.

The room was dark and empty when I looked down. I lay my hand over the glass and tiny cracks began to form. Like a spider web, they expanded out farther and farther until the window was covered. I lifted my hand. The window followed, shard by shard, so slow it was barely moving. I let the glass land on the roof beside me. It didn't make a sound.

I hopped through the skylight and into the massive, empty room. Thirty feet down. Maybe more. I focused just enough to slow my momentum. Perfect. I landed crouching in the center of the council chamber. The soft pad of my feet against the marble floor didn't echo, even in the cavernous space.

A second passed and I was out of the room, sprinting down the hallway to find Avia. The female council members were all in the northeast wing. They were segregated to maintain the appearance of propriety. The thought was laughable to me now.

I had never felt so free and fluid in my movement.

Training with Raelon, even just for the past few weeks, had brought my skill and instinct to a level I had never known possible. I was invisible. I moved through rooms like smoke seeping through the cracks in an old house. There were men standing guard, but they never looked my way.

Avia's apartment was in the far corner of the building. It may have been difficult to find, had it not been marked with her name in gleaming golden letters.

I kneeled, and peered through the little rectangles of glass that framed the door, my face smooshing up against them like a child staring through a bakeshop window. She was not sleeping, but pacing in her room between massive piles of paperwork that leaned ominously to one side or the other. Every now and again, she'd pick something up from one pile, mutter to herself, and replace it on another.

I tiptoed through the shadows, circling the two guards outside her door. They hadn't seen me yet. I was silence and shadow, I told myself. I was smoke.

Across from the bedroom I could see a small kitchen. A pile of dirty dishes had been stacked in the sink. I blinked. The dishes shifted and then toppled, the crash ringing out musically. Their heads all turned towards the sound.

I spun away from the glass just in time to hear their feet pounding by the door as they ran into the kitchen to investigate the sound. The lock to the outer door clicked beneath my open palm and I ran inside the apartment. I was in her bedroom before the door swung shut behind me, its soft sound drawing the eyes of her Ministry Guards. No matter. It would be locked and secure when they approached it to investigate.

"Avia, don't scream. It's Leuka," I whispered from behind her.

She spun around to face me, cheeks red and gasping in the air to release the scream that struggled desperately in her chest. Instead she exhaled a sigh and pulled me into her arms in a strong embrace. I hugged her, my hands sliding up her back to smooth down a matted tangle of her silver-gray hair, usually sleek and neat and tied back tight.

Her hands fell on my shoulders and she took a step back, her red-rimmed eyes meeting my own.

"Come, child. Tell me everything."

"It is as you said," I began. "Everything I knew, it's all lies. They claim they're here to help people. And I believed them. Every word."

Avia took my hand in hers, stilled it. It was only then that I realized it had been shaking.

"It takes a skilled mortician to paint a pretty face on what should be dead and rotten."

"How deep does it go, Avia? The Triad?"

She nodded.

"The Minister?"

She nodded again.

"Chrogus knows what they do. But he only oversees. They pay him off and he keeps his own hands clean. Everyone in the Ministry knows he's not really in charge. It's the three of them. The Triad. They control everything and now that they've got the Silvernail girl, they have infinite financial backing."

She paused, wiping at her nose with her sleeve.

"How could that be? She's only been a councilwoman three months."

"Infinite. Financial. Backing. That's all it took. I've

been living in this shit corner flat twenty years and have never seen the white room. She was inside on her first day."

Her nostrils flared and little flecks of spittle flew from her lips as she spoke.

"They control everything. Have infinite funds. And they want me dead, Avia," I whispered.

She grabbed my hands and squeezed them tightly. "They're not the only ones."

Her tone had changed, and though she was still whispering, the sound of it sent a chill through me so deep I felt it flow through every artery. I was certain my heart would freeze solid and burst into a million jagged, blood-red shards.

She reached behind her to a stack of papers and photographs and grabbed something up.

"The Shadowmen have set a price on your head— retaliation for their defeat. I'm so sorry, dear. He is not what you think."

She handed me the photo. It was black and white, taken in the city that first night. Raelon and me hand in hand as he pulled me forward in the darkness. I could still feel it, the memory of his hand, warm against my own as the rain beat down on us.

"Raelon." I took the photo in my hand, looked at it, my eyes trapped there on his face and refusing to rise up to meet Avia's.

"Raelon," I whispered again, stupidly, but I didn't know what else to say. She didn't understand. She didn't know who he was. If the council had this photo, they must be after him, too. I had to get back to him. Protect him.

She interrupted my frantic thoughts, handing me

another photo, this one from the battle at Hathor. I recognized the man in the picture as the leader from that battle—the wiry frame, the bloody handprint smeared on his face. I had only seen him from afar at the battle. The picture showed his face, his furious beautiful eyes as wide and wild as they had been that first day I saw them in the desert.

"Raelon." My hand went limp and the picture floated to the rich red carpet. I couldn't look at it anymore. "He's not one of them. He doesn't look...I would have recognized a Shadowman."

It didn't make sense.

"A half-breed. That's why they sent him. He looks more like the desert dwellers than his own vile kind. He has been on the Ministry's radar for some time. He would be quite a threat if he were to become their leader. Smart. Tactical."

Her voice sounded muffled and far away. *Half-breed.* He had used that word himself. I felt like I was under water, separated from Avia and her words by a murky ocean.

"This can't be. It's not right. You're wrong," I accused her, but doubt was stabbing my instincts with its dull and rusty blade.

"I've been with him for weeks, alone on an island. Why didn't he kill me already, if that was his goal?"

"A great deal of power stirs inside you, my dear, just swirling at the surface beneath your skin and waiting for someone to pull that trigger. I've known it since I first heard of you. Not as a commander, but as a teenage girl whose rage and sorrow made the trees bow to her in the graveyard as your father was buried. He must have sensed it as well."

I shook my head back and forth. My eyes blurred with tears, but I blinked them away, refusing to let a single one fall. "No. I slept in his arms. He could have killed me and he didn't. He wouldn't."

Avia held out her hand and presented to me a shiny silver sphere. It looked like the round head of a robot. I'd seen one before. They called it a holosphere. She squeezed it in her hand, depressing a round button. When she released her hand, the sphere floated on its own in the air and an image was projected on her wall.

"This was only hours ago, my dear."

Raelon. On our island. He spoke to another man, a Shadowman.

Where is she? Where's the girl?

What do you want with her?

Her head. What else?

The image blurred for a moment.

She's mine. Mine to kill. My mission.

Avia snatched the little ball out of the air and killed the image. "You don't need to see any more of that, dear."

Something deep inside me snapped. Lightning. Electricity. Pain. It was all I felt, surging from my viscera through every nerve ending. Singeing my fingertips, so hot I knew they must be blackened by the energy that shot out of them.

Every window in the room shattered, every glass bauble, every light orb and photo frame. Avia dropped to her knees and covered her head in her arms.

When the shower of glass stopped, she looked up at me, still on her knees. "They'll be coming for you now. Run, child."

I could already hear the two men outside, their boots pounding toward the door. "Scream," I whispered, my voice so cold and hollow I didn't recognize it as my own.

She stared at me for a moment, fear in her eyes. "Scream. Say I broke in the window and tried to turn you to my side. Scream now, or they'll kill you, too."

She stood, took my hand and gave it one final squeeze. Then she screamed a scream so wild it matched her unkempt hair and bloodshot eyes, her voice cracking at the end of it. "She's here. The Lily is here! Help!"

She stared in my eyes, her own wide and dripping. I couldn't see her.

"Run, child. They'll execute you," she whispered.

"They'll try. And I pity them for it. They'll find no mercy here." It didn't sound like my voice. I felt like my soul was shattering, as the windows had. Its jagged pieces flying in every direction and, try as I might, I couldn't make them stop or even slow them down.

The door flew open, Avia's two guards behind it and a dozen running up the stairs behind them. I didn't move. Didn't have to. They stopped. All of them. Still as statues. The effort of movement on each of their grimacing faces, but still they stayed. And would stay until I willed otherwise.

I dove out the window, Avia's fearful cry ringing out as I fell. She didn't know what I could do. I didn't know until that moment. I flipped in the air and slowed my descent seconds before hitting the pavement, landing crouched and ready to attack.

More men waited outside, chiseled angular faces with tan skin and dark hair. Desert dwellers of the Ministry Guard. They were ten yards away and sprinting toward me. This would be too easy. I ran to them. My telekinesis carried me, making each of my light steps supernaturally long and far reaching. I wasn't just running. But I wasn't quite flying.

I reached them in an instant, but did not prepare to defend myself. I didn't have to. I didn't even have to think. My energy had no aim or direction. It simply raged. I moved forward and a path emerged. Men catapulted into the air, into the street, or through windows of nearby buildings. If it was in my way, it was moved. I didn't turn back to see if they were okay. They could have been nursing skinned knees or they could have been a red splatter on a once-clean wall.

I didn't know if any of them would, or even could, follow me. Until I heard the crash. I had never felt so much power, so little control. The buildings on each side of the street collapsed toward me as I ran beneath them. They collided behind me. The snapping of metal beams and stone, shattering glass. It was deafening. Clouds of dust and debris thickened the air, burned my throat and chest as I breathed them in. I couldn't see. I thought they might overtake me, sweep me into the catastrophic mess of my own creation. This thought did not frighten me. But I ran on just the same. The purpose in my mind not to be swayed. One purpose. One light, leading my raging mind on through the darkness and debris surrounding me. Find Raelon. Find him and kill him.

CHAPTER 12

RAELON TOREK

The wind had picked up and sand whipped around me, spiraling up to the graying sky. It came on so fast, so powerful, I thought it might start and never stop. Like the hundred-years storm still raging on the dead Earth. It had only existed for twenty, but experts said it had the power and fuel to rage on for another eighty.

I ran ahead, but the wind slowed me, the sand ground at my skin, and the charcoal sky looming above seemed to whisper horrors into my ears.

I sprinted forward blindly, my eyelids squeezed tight to protect from the constant assault of sand. Each footfall guided only by memory, by instinct. But I stumbled. This storm wasn't nature. Wasn't predictable.

When I felt close I stuck my arms out, feeling for the chipped paint surface and worn wood of the barn door. My body ached from the effort of struggling against the wind. Each step felt like wading through still-wet cement.

Then, finally, I made contact. My hand hit the barn door as I reached forward, expecting it to be farther away. From there I felt my way down to the bottom, slipping my fingers into the crease where wood met sand, and heaved the door up on its rolling track.

"Libby," I yelled. In the seconds my mouth was open to scream her name, a gust of sand forced its way in, rushing down my throat and silencing me. I fell to my knees, trying to cough, to scream, but the air was trapped in my lungs. Fist wrapped around fist, I struck myself hard between the ribs until the gob of sandy spit flung out.

No time to stand. I crawled through the barn door. Inside, the wind felt weaker. I stood and pulled the door back down. The wind and sand whipped against it, relentless. A petulant child banging on a locked door. It moaned and cried and pounded its fists.

I ducked beneath the tail of the rust-bucket spacecraft I'd left hidden there and ran straight for Libby's workshop in the back room. It was empty. Dark. But warm. Several degrees warmer than the rest of the barn. A two-pound hammer lay on the stone floor, a pair of black v-bit tongs beside them, as if cast aside thoughtlessly. Her father's tools. I'd only ever seen them in her hands or hanging on hooks in the wall. She wouldn't have left them like this. Not if she'd had a choice.

I picked up the tongs. They were warm to the touch. In the forge I could see a bit of steel sticking out. I used the tongs to clamp the end and lift it free of the forge. When the steel shifted I could see the hot coal embers glowing red-orange and angry. The steel was heated through. Too hot, the end folding over when I lifted it free. Something had surprised her. She'd left in a hurry.

I dropped the steel back into the forge and ran toward the door.

Outside the storm was still raging. I couldn't open my eyes to look for her. Couldn't open my mouth to call for her. I wasn't going to find her. Not until it was too late.

Then cold fingers wrapped around my ankle. Small fingers. I spun toward the grip, but I could see nothing.

"Raelon. Down here."

Libby. I dropped to all fours patting the sand with my palms until I found her hand again. Her tiny fingers curled around mine and she pulled me forward. I pressed my hand against her cheek, felt her hair fall against it.

"You cut your hair," I said, getting a mouthful of sand.

"Get down here, dumbass." She yelled into my ear. She was below the level of the ground, peeking out from beneath a small wooden door. Her arm shot up quick and the door flung the rest of the way open. I swung my legs around into the little hole and started to climb down.

I was only halfway inside when it stopped. The wind. The noise. All of it. Millions of flying grains of sand froze in mid-air for a fraction of a second and fell back to the ground. I looked around the desert. I could see the sand still flying yards away from us, as if we were watching it from a window. We were in the eye of the storm. I climbed the rest of the way out of the open hatch.

Libby crawled out behind me and hopped to her feet.

"Quick, attack before they recover," she screamed down the hole.

"Attack who?"

"Shadowmen. At least six, maybe more. They came out of nowhere. The storm gave us cover and we hid underground."

I recognized some of the men and women from the underground camp when they filed out of the hatch. Only now they looked like soldiers. Moved like soldiers. They were bolting across the newly placid desert, weapons at the ready.

"How did she find out?" Libby asked.

"What are you talking about?"

She grabbed the front of my shirt in both hands and shook me.

"Wake up, Rae. This is her. Have you ever heard the story of Blue Victoria?"

I stared at her blankly. "Blue what?"

"Little Fehr girl that saw her family murdered? Kid had so much rage in her she caused the biggest sandstorm this desert had ever seen. *Telekinetic event*, that's what the skyboards called it. More like a power surge, though. Ripped through her so hard her hair turned blue, hence the name."

Her soldiers were already attacking, swift and graceful like birds of prey. No mercy was shown to my one-time Shadowmen brothers. They were new to combat. But they'd had a good teacher. They killed two right away, caught off guard and still struggling to get to their feet.

"You're saying Leuka is having some sort of power surge and causing this?"

She whacked me on the forehead with her open palm.

"Duh. And I'm willing to bet you're to blame."

There wasn't time. Two Shadowmen were already rushing us. I kept close to Libby. My gut churned out loud. It felt wrong to face my own blood with my weapon drawn. I should be among them.

"Damn you for bringing this upon us, Raelon. In case you don't remember, we've already got a war to fight.

What do these assholes want?" Libby yelled.

"Me," I whispered. "And Leuka. They know about us."

I turned from her to meet the attack coming directly from behind me. I didn't recognize him at first. One of Moses's assassins; Hogo, I think was his name. He hurled himself at me clumsily and I stabbed him through the neck with a single swift sword stroke. Blood ran down the blade and hilt, drops rolling onto my fingers and slipping between my knuckles and wetting the little hairs on my arm. I stared at him, stuck on my blade and I couldn't move. I didn't want to be this anymore. This killer. This monster.

Libby took a big stomp forward, jumped high and kicked the body so it slid back off my sword.

"Thanks."

"Sure."

"Hey, Lib."

"Yeah?"

"What happened to Blue Victoria?"

"Soul sickness. Like most pales, she couldn't handle feeling that much all at once. I heard she died."

I froze. Leuka was here. I felt her before I saw her—at the far corner where the storm met stillness. I looked, just to confirm my instinct, to feed my eyes with the sight of her. Her face was gray, eyes red. Something was wrong. I was sprinting toward her before Libby's words could register in my brain.

"Raelon, don't," she called but it was too late.

I took no more than two steps before I flew backward, smashing through the sun-softened wood of the barn and slamming into something metal and unyielding. I bounced off it and landed on the stone floor of the barn.

My ship.

A fist slammed into my jaw and I felt a pop as it dislocated. The Shadowman behind the fist must have been inside already when I crashed through the wall, taking cover from the sandstorm.

I fell to my knees with my head in both hands and jerked it back into place. My scream was involuntary. A product of the pain. Then a foot was flying at my face. I hadn't had enough time to recover. I fell awkwardly to the side, the kick missing by no more than a centimeter.

I was on my back. Not a place you wanted to be in any kind of fight. The nameless warrior tried to kick me again, this time aiming at the ribs below my left armpit. I caught him by his poorly crafted leather boot and yanked him down to my level. On my feet in a second, I grabbed the young warrior by his neck and threw him out of my way. No time for these peons. I had to get to Leuka.

I barreled out of the barn but she was gone.

"Leuka," I called out to the sand and sky.

"Hello, Lover." It was her voice, but twisted and wrong. She was perched atop the barn, crouched like some desert beast, lean and coiled with eyes full of violence. I cried out in fear when she sprung up and dove at the ground head first, but she slowed down in mid-air and flipped onto her feet a second before impact.

She was stomping toward me. I tried to speak, but she snapped her fist closed and the air drained from my lungs like a popped balloon. I couldn't take a breath. Couldn't make a sound.

"Turn around."

I didn't understand.

She rolled her eyes, swatted the air, and I flipped around with my back to her. I didn't know she had this kind of power, had never seen anything like it.

She grabbed the back of my shirt in both hands and ripped it off me.

As she screamed, the air rushed back into my chest and I fell to my knees sucking in air like I'd been drowning. Her scream shook me. The sand vibrated beneath my feet with the pain and anger in that long guttural cry.

She ran her finger over the scars on my back.

"You were planning to kill me? Why don't you go ahead and try?"

I was still on my knees, gasping in the sand.

"You wanted to kill me, right? Go ahead, here's your chance. Or were you going to wait until I couldn't fight back? Until I was naked and curled up asleep in your arms?"

"Leuka, no," I tried to explain but she snapped her fist closed and I couldn't breathe again.

"No more lies, half-shadow."

She threw me across the desert. I landed hard on my back in the sand, the air rushing out of me with the impact. It was a moment before I could even gasp in a desperate mouthful of air. Tiny black spots started appearing, floating around my field of vision. My fault. All of this. My fault.

THE END